SYNERGY

SYNERGY

Rosemary I. Patterson, Ph.D.

To order additional copies of this book, contact:
Xlibris Corporation
1-888-7-XLIBRIS
www.Xlibris.com
Orders@Xlibris.com

CONTENTS

CHAPTER 1.

A Pressing Problem.

"On a one-to-ten, this is a ten-plus day," Fila Enderby said to her executive secretary Alvin, as they jogged along the wooden walkway next to Laguna Beach. Fila stared at the white-caps on the turquoise water off California with approval.

"If only my employees can manage to function on their own in the office, Alvin."

Fila appreciated that the wind was keeping pollution away, and that the recent rains were turning the iron-woods, palms and hibiscus bushes back into their verdant green.

"Oh, the employees will manage somehow, darling," Alvin said sarcastically. His tone irritated Fila. "Remember what's really important in this world," he added. "Running the Los Angeles marathon in style, but how you're going to do that in that outfit is beyond me."

Alvin glanced at Fila's basic sports top and running shorts in dismay.

"After all, darling, you are the most successful real estate entrepreneur in all of Orange County. Surely you could reflect more of your success in the clothes you wear?"

"Alvin, that's all you care about, how you look?" she protested. Fila glanced at Alvin's chic jogging outfit and trendy sunglasses in irritation.

"But of course, darling? How else am I going to attract the love of my life? And if you ask me, you should be doing the same. If you want to please your father before he dies, that is."

Alvin's words brought back Fila's most pressing problems. She felt herself lose her customary, smooth, jogging gait as anger and pain towards her only surviving parent flooded through her usually business-focused mind.

Fila went back in her mind to the sequence of events that had brought her to the lowest moment in her life. Fila remembered that she had been present in the doctor's office when her father was given a death sentence. He had been told that he had less than a year to live.

Fila had thought that her father would at least try and enjoy the little time he had left and turn Enderby Developments over to her to run. After all, she had already been managing all the company's projects in Orange County, California.

Instead, her father had ordered her to find a husband capable of running Enderby Developments and, of all things, to get pregnant before his death to produce the grandson who would carry on the Enderby genetic line.

And as if that wasn't enough for Fila to cope with, he had launched into a severe criticism of her handling of her latest and most important Orange County project. His words came back to her.

"I want you to stop the takeover of that Seniors' Complex, Fila. Every talk show and newspaper column in this state is calling you the Leona Helmsley of Orange County."

All because a few pensioners had complained that they would have nowhere to go if she bulldozed their decrepit, old senior citizens' residence. Fila went into a frenzy of emotion as she remembered.

"I can't believe it. Alvin," she blurted. "Why father was the one who taught me to ignore bleeding hearts and compassionate causes."

"Well, don't tie yourself up in a knot, darling," Alvin's words whipped up even more emotion. "That won't attract the love of your life at all. Believe me, I know. What you really need is a complete makeover. Why, those dreadful shorts you're wearing are creeping right up your crotch, for heaven's sake. And the Los Angeles marathon is only two weeks away."

"Alvin, there's more to life than marathons," she shouted, pulling her shorts down.

"And those shoes." Alvin glared at her cross-trainers in despair. "Basic white, if I'm not mistaken. Don't you realize the world has gone psychedelic?"

"Alvin!" she screamed. "My father is dying from lung cancer. I have to marry and produce a child pronto if I want to become the next chief executive officer of Enderby Developments. My greatest business accomplishment is about to be shot down by grey-power activists and all you can think of is looking good in a marathon."

"What can you expect from someone whose mother named him after a chipmunk? Lighten up, believe me, the only way out of your predicament is to attract a man as quickly as you can. Do you want the name of my beautician? I'm sure she can do wonders for you, too."

"There must be another way," Fila shot back. She thought deeply about her predicament. "Imagine my father changing his will to read that the first of his children to produce a male heir will inherit the controlling interest of Enderby Developments," she complained again to Alvin.

Fila thought of her brother Drew. Her mother had unexpectedly died when Drew was ten and Fila was 16, and since then her brother had sought a surrogate. He had devoted himself to pursuing first teenagers, and now middle-aged women years older than himself.

"Now I have to marry and become pregnant or there's a chance that the dweeb of a brother of mine will take over as chief executive officer after father's death instead of me," she seethed.

"Well, I must admit, your father's new will is a shocker. And you do have the strangest brother. Isn't this the third lawsuit brought against him for alienation of affections? Can't he chase unmarried women, for heaven's sake."

"Drew prefers older women, Alvin."

"But I will never marry," she vowed. "Men are always viewing me as a gravy train or wanting to use me as a stepping-stone to power."

"You do have the strangest problems, I must admit, darling. I only wish handsome men were willing to use me as a gravytrain or a stepping-stone. I'd be only to happy to oblige."

"Alvin," she protested. "Be serious."

"You know, darling, the will doesn't say anything about marrying. It just stipulates that a living male heir must exist. May be there's some way you can just have a child. Like Madonna," he advised.

"If Madonna can find some fellow with a high sperm count and good genetics, jogging in some park, you should be able do do the same. You are wealthy, young and beautiful, you know. Particularly, if you would take my advice and have a complete makeover."

"Alvin, be serious," she ordered him. "I've got all these problems and all you can do is joke."

"I'm not joking. I'm quite serious. It could work, you know. Think about it. Draw up a quick list of attributes you would want in the father of your child."

"Alvin," she protested.

"Don't be too fussy, darling. Remember time is of the essence." Fila ignored his sarcasm.

"Euro-American background, college or better education, an indication of giftedness of some kind, classic good looks, strong physique, above-average height, no evidence of balding in the family line, and, most important of all, willingness to procreate and then fade from the scene."

"Now you're getting the idea, darling," Alvin encouraged as Fila slowed her jogging pace and started to look at the men on the beach.

"I must be losing my rational mind, Alvin," she protested. "What you're proposing is starting to make sense to me."

Alvin pointed at a man jogging towards them in the distance. Fila looked but quickly realised that the fellow was on a skateboard and was carrying the largest boom box she had ever seen in his hands. Her ears were nearly deafened as the young fellow went by.

"I hope you can find someone more suitable than him," Fila ordered.

"Of course," he pronounced. "Really, darling, you don't pay me enough for all I do for you."

"You can get pregnant, you know, if that's what it's going to take to become CEO. You could have some legally binding contract drawn up that would give you the right to the child, forever. Just like Madonna did."

"Alvin, you're too much," she protested. "Will you be serious?"

"May be he would do?" Alvin pointed as they jogged around a corner and came into viewing distance of a man. Fila stared in the direction Alvin was pointing.

"Alvin," she gasped. "That man has tattoos all over his body and he's jogging with a pitbull."

"Well, if you're going to be fussy, this might take a while. How about that one over there, against that boat." Fila followed Alvin's directions.

A large-framed, still youngish man with classic good looks and a full head of golden hair, was strumming a guitar and singing on the beach next to the sea walk.

"Oh, he's gorgeous, darling," Alvin encouraged.

Fila pointed to the hat from which the man appeared to be soliciting donations.

"Well, may be he's not perfect, but time is running short. May be that means that the Greek Adonis would be likely to accept a monetary proposition from you with a legal agreement limiting the amount of separation allowance and access to any offspring?"

"Don't be ridiculous, Alvin."

Fila's secretary pulled her down onto the grass just close enough to take a closer look at the fellow Alvin had just spotted. Despite herself, she ran her eyes over the man in her customary evaluative manner. After all, her father had trained her in the "eyeball" test for assessing human potential.

"He's perfect," Alvin pronounced. "I could certainly get it on with him, myself. Look at his muscles. And his hair looks like it's been professionally styled. He even dresses well, that is, if you don't mind a casual emphasis. Why, that man can even sing."

Fila strained her ears to listen closely.

"Save the whales and the dolphins," the man sang in perfect pitch.

"Oh, my God, he must be a bleeding-heart environmentalist," Fila groaned.

"Well, I'm sure that activism can't be passed on genetically, darling."

"And he's straight and doesn't seem to be married?" Alvin noted.

"How can you tell?" Fila gasped.

"Trust me darling. I have a natural radar for this type of thing."

"Nice day?" Fila turned beet red as the attractive singer put down his guitar and came over to speak to them.

Fila decided that he had a strong chin line. She noted that her heart rate involuntarily sped up as the man gave her a warm smile and put out his hand. Fila noted that his face was perfectly symmetrical."

"Rolf Nordquist," he introduced himself. "Couldn't help but notice your interest," he added.

"Toodle oo," Alvin told Fila as he shook Rolf Nordquist's hand.

"Alvin, you can't leave me now," she protested.

"Sorry, darling! I've just remembered a workout appointment? Lovely chap visiting from the East Coast. Could be my soulmate. Let me know how you make out."

"Rolf Nordquist?" Fila questioned, trying to capture a semblance of her rational mind. For some reason, Alvin's outrageous solution to her problem was starting to sound plausible. She decided that it must be desperation.

"Isn't that a Norwegian name?"

"Right on," he replied.

Alvin's list of attributes flowed into Fila's mind.

"Norwegian, that's Euro-American, isn't it?"

"Right. I'm second generation American, though. My great-grandfather came to America on a fishing vessel. Who are you?"

"Fila Enderby," she introduced herself.

He whistled. "Fila Enderby, the evil vice-president of Enderby Developments that's determined to evict those nice pensioners from their seniors' complex so she can flip the land under it for an indecent profit? I don't believe it. You don't look at all like what I thought Fila Enderby would look like. I imagined you as much older and much less shapely." Rolf looked at her physical attributes with approval.

Fila realized Rolf must have been watching the television coverage of the whining pensioners.

"Oh, that's just a bunch of media hype," she lied. "We will relocate everyone of those sweet pensioners before we bulldoze that old building. To somewhere much nicer than where they are now."

"Well in that case, can I buy you some lunch?" Rolf asked startling Fila further with the warmth in his voice.

"Oh, don't worry, I don't always beg on the beach," he assured her. "I'm just trying to finance my latest CD. It's dedicated to saving the last of the rainforest in the Amazon. I've set up a foundation to save the land next to the Yanomami reservation in Jaranei, Brazil. Any profits from my latest CD will go towards more land purchases. My foundation already has 10,000 acres in trust for the Yanomami."

"Isn't putting out a CD a rather chancy way to raise money?"

Rolf told her how generous people at Laguna Beach could be, when they knew the money was for a generous cause.

"My regular gigs give me enough to live on but I have to raise extra funds to finance my pet projects. And middle-aged ladies along Laguna Beach are always so generous to me. As you can see." Rolf went over and scooped up the large pile of tens and twenties from his hat.

"I've dedicated my life to saving the Yanomami," he explained. "Any time, I need extra funds to purchase more land I just resort to serenading the older ladies."

"Funny, I was just going to offer you lunch," Fila stated. On the spur of the moment she had decided to pursue Alvin's plan.

"It must be the sun," she told herself. Suddenly, Alvin's advice seemed workable.

"Oh, anyone as attractive as you doesn't need to subsidize me," Rolf Nordquist promised warmly. "Believe me, I always have a little set aside to romance anyone I find especially attractive. Even if you are the 'Leona Helmsley' of Laguna Beach the media is making you out to be."

"What do you mean?"

"I believe in synergy," he explained. "Being in contact with others with opposing views to your own. That way, both people have an opportunity to expand their horizons."

"How about the pizza restaurant that's just down the street," Rolf suggested to Fila's dismay. She quelled her misgivings and nodded. She hated fast food restaurants. Fila customarily ate lunch in only four or five-star rated ones. But her despair had lessened somewhat as she realised she was seriously considering Alvin's advice.

"May be there is a solution to my most pressing problem," she thought.

She decided that Rolf Nordquist must be from hippie-ville but that Alvin was probably right that he needed money. On the spot, Fila decided that it wouldn't be too hard to get him into the sack. She knew she didn't mean to make the arrangement permanent, anyway. Fila repressed her dislike of social activists.

CHAPTER 2.

Rolf Nordquist.

I can't believe my luck, I mused as I placed my arm firmly around the shoulder of my new found acquaintance, Fila Enderby, one of the wealthiest women of Orange County, and shepherded her over to the pizza place.

I think she's sympathetic to my project to save the Amazon rainforest and the Yanomami, I decided, ignoring the lady's slight look of distaste as we entered the pizza restaurant. I didn't think she hung out at fast food restaurants much, I chuckled to myself. But my first priority was to check out just how much the wealthy lady was attracted to me.

On an attraction scale of one to ten, I would say she's close to a ten, I decided, noting Fila attempting to hide her look of revulsion at the decor of the pizza place.

I had better sweet-talk this woman into something special, I warned myself. I need another 13,000 for my new CD by Friday at the latest or the deal is off. There's no hope I can collect that much from infatuated, matronly donors so quickly. I can't believe discs cost $14,000 to produce at the minimum these days.

Oh, there's my little buddy, Zot, I sensed an opportunity to check out the level of Fila Enderby's infatuation further. If the lady isn't highly attracted I'm going to have to dump her quick, I told myself, even if I do find her quite personally attractive. I noted my own attraction with surprise.

It's not often that I find flirting with these wealthy Orange County matrons pleasant, I thought, but this one is still young and very beautiful. I mentally reminded myself that my first prioriy was my Amazon CD.

I led the lady over to a rather slight, oriental man in his twenties wearing glasses with thick lenses. Zot was wearing his usual cherry-red and orange robes. He was sitting by himself in one of the large nooks overlooking the bay. An anguished look appeared for a second or two on Fila's face but she quickly changed it to a forced smile.

I imagine she's reacting to Zot's shaven head, I thought. I'm on a roll for sure, my spirits picked up considerably as I anticipated the look of pleasure on the face of the manager of the recording studio.

She's a ten plus for sure, I gloated. I detected a slight gasp as the lady was forced to sit down between Zot and myself.

"Zot, this is Ms. Fila Enderby. She's a real estate tycoon. Tell her what you do," I ordered.

"Tycoon? Wat tycoon," Zot asked.

"Tycoon sell land, buildings, Zot, on large scale."

"How you do?" Zot bowed politely and spoke in his fractured English. "I Lama Tsot Rinpoche."

"A pleasure, I'm sure," the lady answered. "Tell me what is a llama? I thought they were an animal species from South America." Fila looked perplexed.

"Not sentient being kind llama, South America. Buddhist kind Lama, from Tibet," Zot said.

"Zot is a holy man," I explained. "From Tibet."

"At his age? Why, he's not more than 25 if he's a day."

I related how Zot had spent his life since he was five years old studying in a monastery. I told Fila that Zot was recognized as an incarnation of a great master who had died, and that really dedicated incarnation monks who are brought to monasteries as young as four can reach the status of a Lama in their twenties if they work hard.

"Lama Tsot work hard fo sure," Zot emphasized. "In West, may be study 18 years, include university, become Doctor. Same Tibet. Study since five years of age."

"Whatever has brought you to Laguna Beach, Lama Zot?" Fila Enderby asked, sounding rather worried.

"His Holiness send Laguna Beach," Zot explained. "Say must go to West. Sacred duty preserve Tibetan Buddhist religion. Chinese destroy religion, culture in Tibet. His Holiness set up Dharma Centers in West. No more room monks, Lamas, Dharamsala."

"His Holiness? Dharma Center? Dharamsala?" Fila Enderby looked even more confused.

"The Dalai Lama," I explained. I gave Fila a short lecture about him. I told her that he was the exiled spiritual leader of Tibet who had been given the Nobel Peace Prize for his non-violent resistance against China's invasion of his country. I explained that a Dharma Center is a center for practicing and studying of Tibetan Buddhist principles, and that Dharamsala is where the Dalai Lama hangs out. I told Fila that over 90,000 Tibetan refugees live in a tiny part of India now with the Dalai Lama. My voice rose with concern as I told her that there was no room for any more, and that new refugees, even children, that kept escaping through mountain passes in the winter had to be sent somewhere else or back to Tibet.

"Center fo Sangha," Zot added. Fila stared non-comprehendingly at him again. I could tell she was having enormous difficulty understanding his attempts at English. "You know," Zot looked desperate. "Sangha, like community fo Christian Church, only community study Buddhism."

"That's one of the things I admire about Zot," I told Fila. "I've been trying to help him learn English. He's only been in an English speaking country for a month but does he ask me how to translate simple words or phrases like 'coffee' and 'where is the bus?' No way. He asks me words like 'community' and 'sentient being.' Why, some of the words he asked me to translate I have had to look up in the dictionary and I've been to university."

"Zot may have been educated in a Third World monastery," I testified, "but the philosophical education he received sure wasn't third rate."

"Whatever did you study in university, Mr. Nordquist?"

"Music and philosophy," I replied. I avoided telling Fila Enderby that I had also studied business but had found it extremely lacking after discovering Buddhist philosophy. The lady nodded.

"You want to set up a Buddhist center in Orange County, Lama Zot?" Fila Enderby sounded shocked to the core. I smiled. I decided that Fila was anticipating real estate values dropping at a rapid pace.

"What would you like for lunch?" I asked my new acquaintance, encouraged further that she wasn't walking out the door in a huff.

A ten plus, I congratulated myself. Usually, it took several hours and occasionally, even days before a female object of my attention became convinced I was their long-lost soulmate.

"Their 'Maui Cheese Bonanza' pizza is delicious," I recommended.

"Maui Cheese Bonanza pizza? Just exactly what's in it? Oh never mind, whatever you're having will be fine," she almost stammered. I suspected the lady had never been inside a pizza place before.

"What about you Zot?" I offered. I knew my Tibetan buddy didn't have one cent to his name.

"Zot's luck hasn't been too good, lately," I explained. "The Dalai Lama financed the set up of the Dharma Center but several of the local thugs relieved Zot of the bank draft he was carrying the first night he got here."

"Dey got passport, visa and green card Dalai Lama got fo me, too," Zot explained. He pointed to the stitches in his head. "Rolf take hospital, save life." Zot gave me a look of pure gratitude.

"I found him lying next to the wooden sidewalk." I explained. "Unconscious. Had to pay up front for his medical care, before the ambulance would take him to the hospital. Wiped me right out. Seems the local cops don't believe Zot that he's in the country legally. I tried to notify the Tibetan officals in Dharamsala where the Dalai Lama lives, sent them a fax followed by a letter, but so far we haven't got a reply. Zot's only got another month and the County officials are going to deport him if he can't prove he's here legally," I explained.

"What an interesting life you lead, Mr. Nordquist," Fila Enderby remarked.

"Please call me Rolf, Fila," I ordered in my most encouraging voice. The lady gave me an evaluative look.

"You do someting help Lama Tsot," Zot looked at Fila Enderby pleadingly. "Rolf say you typhoon. Good karma, help Buddhist Lama. Earn much merit fo next lifetime."

"Tycoon, Zot, not typhoon," I corrected.

"Karma, next lifetime?" Fila said, looking perplexed again.

"We'll discuss it later, Zot," I ordered. "What will you have for lunch?"

"Maui Cheese Bonanza, tanks, Rolf."

I went over to the counter and ordered the works, bonanzas, shakes and three banana splits.

I decided that my chances of raising the thirteen grand were looking up. I realised that the lady didn't leave even with Zot hitting on her for help.

I made several trips back to the table with the food and enjoyed myself immensely as Fila Enderby forced herself to eat what I was sure was not her ordinary diet.

I bet she's using up her entire month's quota of salt, fat, cholesterol, sugar and white flour, I laughed to myself. I noticed Zot gulping down his meal ravenously.

"That shelter I got you in feeding you all right, Zot?" I questioned.

"Have go elsewhere," Zot confessed.

"Why Zot?" I asked suspiciously. "What happened this time?" It was the third shelter he had been kicked out of in two weeks.

"Center no allow prostrations. Others no like Tibetan chant, drum, cymbals. Need burn candles, chant, make offerings Buddhas. Need help."

"Prostrations?" Fila queried. "Is that some kind of quirky, religious, sexual thing."

I laughed. "No, you've probably heard ignorant references to tantric practices."

"You tried to burn candles at that shelter, Zot," I groaned. "You know matches and fires of any kind are strictly forbidden. I thought of the ramshackle wooden structure I had taken Zot to.

"It's a wonder that place didn't go up in flames."

"Zot come live wit Rolf?" he asked plaintively.

"No, Zot not come live wit Rolf," I answered. "My landlord gave me till five o'clock today to clean my own things out of his place. He's conservative with a big "C". When he heard me singing that Hawaiian sovereignty movement song by Keali'i Reichel, he threw my favorite electric guitar right into the goldfish pond and ordered me out. How was I supposed to know that his company just invested heavily in land development on Maui?"

"There's a sovereignty movement in Hawaii?" Fila Enderby looked horrified.

"You do somting?" Zot queried Fila again. "Help Lama Tsot? Help Rolf? He environmental activist, try help all sentient beings. Good Karma, you help?"

Fila gave Zot a long appraising look like she was carefully weighing something. I cringed.

Damn that Zot, I thought. Just when I had this lady eating out of my hand. Now he's gone and blown the whole thing by hitting so strongly on her too soon.

"Mr. Nordquist, I would like to talk to you privately?" Fila confirmed my fears. She's gone back to Mr. Nordquist, I thought. And she's talking to me like I'm one of her employees or something.

"Zot, get lost for 10 minutes," I ordered. "Don't worry. We'll find someplace for the night," I promised. "Wait for me outside."

Zot clambered to his feet.

"Nice meet you, Ms. Enderbly," he bowed.

"Enderby," I shouted. "Fila Enderby." Zot moved to the exit. I prepared to kiss my hopes for my Amazon disc goodbye as I tried to apologize for Zot.

"Sorry about Zot hitting on you like that, Fila," I tried my most pleasant manner. "He doesn't realize how things are done in America? In Tibetan Buddhist countries, locals always give food and shelter to Lamas. They consider it a meritorious thing to do."

"How do you know so much about Tibetan Buddists, Mr. Nordquist?" Fila demanded.

"Been studying Buddhism for many years. I even studied under several Buddhist masters in Nepal," I explained. "In the eighties. I was at a center set up by a venerable Lama who had had to flee Tibet when the Chinese invaded."

"Just how old are you, Mr. Nordquist?"

"Oh, I was just a youth when I was in Nepal," I countered. There was no way I was going to reveal to Fila Enderby that I was probably a number of years older than her.

"Tell me, Mr. Nordquist," the lady sounded very serious. "Just how anxious are you to finance that CD of yours? And to get some help for Lama Zot. I might be able to help financially and find a place where you and your mysterious Lama friend could live?"

"Very anxious," I admitted. I thought about how the Yanomami were running out of time and how the West desperately needed more Buddhist centers.

"I want to hire you for several months, Mr. Nordquist," Fila Enderby explained. I nearly passed out with shock.

"Or until we achieve what I'm going to contract with you to do," she added. "I will need you constantly at my beck and call, night and day at certain, sensitive times. Would 15,000 dollars a month be enough? And a residence where you, Lama Zot, and myself can stay. My father's summer residence at Newport Beach should do, I think."

I sensed an advantage.

"Night and day. That's pretty restrictive," I commented. "I do have gigs pre-booked."

"Then cancel them," Fila ordered.

"You'll guarantee Zot will be allowed to stay in California," I bargained.

"That's against my better judgement, Mr. Nordquist, but if you insist, I'll contact a friend of mine is the Immigration Department."

"And you'll let him carry on his Buddhist activities in your father's summer home and finance the start-up of a Dharma Center somewhere in Laguna Beach."

"Somewhere in Orange County, Mr. Nordquist; Laguna Beach may have restrictive covenances in its zoning."

"Plus another month's wages as a bonus if you're satisfied with my work?"

The lady looked rather coldly at me.

"You drive a hard bargain, Mr. Nordquist. But I'm under considerable time pressure. I'll agree to your terms."

"You need someone killed?" I gasped, realising how much the lady was offering. "Buddhists are not supposed to kill, not even fish."

"No, killing won't be required," Fila gave a short laugh. "Quite the opposite, actually. I had better elaborate, I think. Promise me that you will keep everything I say in confidence."

"Of course," I promised.

"I find myself in a very embarrasing position, Mr. Nordquist. I don't want to go into details but it's imperative that I become impregnated immediately. I want to hire you to assure that the goal gets accomplished as soon as possible. Do you think such a thing is within your ability? Be honest if you would find such an undertaking offensive?"

"Impregnate you?" I whistled. "Are you serious?"

Fila Enderby turned beet red. I picked up her racing emotions.

She really is desperate, I detected. My chakra balancing meditation I learned in Tibet and practiced daily resulted in my being rather psychic.

"I assure you I wouldn't find that job description offensive at all," I reassured the lady.

It must be her biological time-clock ticking, I thought. She doesn't look nearly that age but I suppose it happens to some women early.

"I'm not looking for anything permanent, Mr. Nordquist," Fila Enderby warned. "Once our goal is accomplished I would want no further contact with you or of you with any offspring. Is that understood?"

"You want to use me as a sperm bank? I've heard of woman doing that but I never expected to meet one."

"Precisely. You are free of genetic defects, I presume?"

"As far as I'm aware," I assured her.

"I'll have a legal agreement drawn up, then and a cheque authorized in your name?" I thought of the Yanomami again and Zot's Dharma Center."

"Fifteen thousand in advance?" I queried, thinking of my payment due Friday.

"As you wish," she replied.

I put out my hand. She shook it firmly. I could feel her hand trembling slightly.

"You and Lama Tsot can accompany me to my car, Mr. Nordquist," my generous new benefactor ordered. "I'll help you pick up your belongings from your landlord's house immediately." The lady's tone of voice brooked no answering back.

"Given what you're contracting to happen I insist you call me Rolf," I said as I moved towards the exit, my head reeling.

And I thought she was enamored with my personality, I mused, and it's only my body she's interested in.

CHAPTER 3.

Geoffrey Enderby.

Why has God punished me by taking my wife, leaving me with my relationship-challenged offspring and now cutting short my life? I cursed. I forced myself to ignore the savage pain in my lungs and respiratory region. Breathing was becoming harder and harder. I glanced in the mirror. My summer residence housekeeper was coming to tell me something she considered urgent about my daughter and I didn't want her to notice the deterioration in my physical appearance since I saw her last. Mrs. McMaster had been with our family for many years.

I'm getting to be an expert make up artist, I decided, as I applied the cover-up that kept everyone around me from realising how quickly.I was going downhill with the lung cancer that had struck me out of nowhere. A wan smile covered my face as the dark shadows under my eyes and my deeply entrenched facial and neck wrinkles disappeared with the ease of a brush stroke. My new, designer clothes, five sizes below what I ordinarily wore, kept the huge amount of weight I had lost from showing. My thoughts went back to what Mrs. McMaster had said about my daughter.

"Having an affair with a weirdo activist," had been her exact words.

It couldn't be, I thought. Why, Fila had a history of running from eligible members of the opposite sex, much to my irritation. I flipped on my intercom to my secretary.

"Summon Alvin Carstairs," I ordered my secretary. "Right now, before Mrs. McMaster gets here."

Within minutes, there was a knock on my door. I pressed the switch that opened it.

"You summoned, Geoffrey?" Fila's long-time secretary cautiously crept into my office. I motioned him to a seat in front of my desk. His calling me by my first name always irritated me but I realised that this was no time to attempt to put the fellow in his place. Next to me, Carstairs knew more about my daughter than any other living human. She had brought him into the company when she graduated from business school with a masters degree.

"What do you know about my daughter's love life, Carstairs?" He looked shocked and then defensive.

"Why, only what you've always confided in me, Geoffrey. That both your children are relationship-challenged, I believe you told me."

"That's right," I sighed. "Drew has always been impossible; he's an impulsive and uncontrollable older woman chaser, but I had such high hopes for Fila. Thought she would marry someone just like me one day. Someone that could guide this company into the next millenium. And provide a grandson or grandsons that could keep Enderby Developments going even longer."

"Well, I'm sure she will, Geoffrey," Carstairs replied. "In confidence, I know Fila is working on it but these things do take time, you know."

"No, Carstairs. God gave me a daughter who flees at the very sight of talented businessmen. God knows, I've introduced her to enough of them. I wonder what's the matter with her. May be she's a lesbian, for God's sake?" The thought sent me into a vicious coughing fit.

"Really, Geoffrey. It wouldn't be the end of the world if she was, I assure you. The world is a different place than it was when you were growing up, you know."

"Carstairs! I didn't call you in here to discuss your views on same-sex relationships. I just want to find out who my daughter has been seeing lately? I'm sure you must know. She tells you everything."

"Well, Fila does tell me that I'm indispensible, Geoffrey, but I don't have a clue who she's been dating, I assure you. I just got back this morning from the east coast. A well-deserved holiday with such a nice chap, I assure you. One of those brief but intense flirtations. I had hopes for more but it was evident that the fellow was too superficial for me."

"Carstairs, I'm not interested in your love life. I want to know who my daughter is dating, if anyone."

"Geoffrey, I haven't even seen your daughter yet. She's not in the office at the moment."

Something in the man's manner made me suspicious. He lacked some of his usual self-confidence.

"Carstairs, my summer home housekeeper, Mrs. McMaster tells me that my daughter is having an affair with some weirdo activist. Can you shed any light on this matter?"

"Oh, she must be talking about that gorgeous folk-singer Fila and I met while jogging on Laguna Beach, Geoffrey, before I went back east. I had hopes for that relationship. But that man is not a weirdo activist, I assure you. He's a fairly well known country music artist. Absolutely, devastatingly handsome. And quite successful, I assure you."

"My daughter is having an affair with a county music singer?" I choked. It was becoming harder and harder to breathe.

"Well, I certainly don't know about that, Geoffrey," Carstairs replied. "The last time I saw Fila she was just checking the man out."

"That's enough, Carstairs. I'll get to the bottom of this, I assure you. And don't you dare say anything about this to my daughter, understand?"

I called my secretary in. I knew better than to let Carstairs go unescorted back to his office. The first thing he would do is place a call to Fila.

"Lucille, take Carstairs and give him a personal tour of our new office wing," I ordered.

"The new office wing in La Jolla, Mr. Enderby?"

"Yes, take today and tomorrow, if necessary. And don't let Carstairs, out of your sight, understand?"

"Really, Geoffrey," Carstairs protested. I waved them both out of my sight.

These attacks get worse all the time, I gasped as my body went into a state of uncontrollable choking and retching. I unlocked my desksafe and shakily reached for the morphine I kept hidden from prying eyes.

This is all that's keeping me going, I realised as I injected the pain-stopping liquid into my distended veins. Thank God, the company doctor keeps me well supplied.

I'II have to change my will again, I mused darkly, before it's too late. Fila's been furious with me ever since I changed it the first time. But neither Drew or Fila have done anything so far to arrange suitable marriages.

I'll not leave Enderby Developments in the hands of either one of my children, I vowed. Time is running short and both of them have massive relationship problems, I realized. Drew is a compulsive older woman chaser and Fila up until now has been a hermit. After all, I did make that promise to my own father when he willed me the company.

"Promise me, that you will evaluate your own children thoroughly, Geoff," father had begged me on his deathbed. Drew had only been six at the time and Fila not much older.

"If Drew is not prize management material and/or Fila has married unwisely, consider setting up a private trust to oversee the business. That way, you can obtain the best in management people. Remember, the survival of Enderby Developments is more important than being kind to your offspring if they are not suitable. Good genetic material runs in the Enderby lineage and sooner or later an Enderby worthy of top management will emerge. Until then, a trust will preserve the assets."

That's what I'll have to do if what Mrs. McMaster or Carstairs says is true, I thought seriously. Fila having an affair with some long-haired activist, and/or a country music artist.

But that couldn't be, why she's a God damned hermit, for heaven's sake. God knows I've stalled as long as I can.

My summer home, filled with hippies, Mrs. McMaster claims. Lighting incense and chanting in some foreign language. She must be mistaken. But she says she's got the photographs to prove it.

The buzzer on my desk went off interrupting my thoughts.

"Mrs. McMaster is here to see you, Mr. Enderby," my other secretary announced. I glanced one more time into the mirror. I felt some relief as the mirror reflected a still handsome, slightly grey-haired, middle-aged executive, the recent white in my hair covered by a competent hairdresser. I flipped the button that unlocked my office.

"Welcome Mrs. McMaster," I greeted the old warhorse. She looked at me closely.

"Your daughter told me you were very ill, Mr. Enderby, but you look quite well to me."

"Family always exaggerate these things," I lied, grateful that my make up was so effective.

"What is it you wanted to show me, Mrs. McMaster?" I got right to the point.

"It's those hippies, Mr. McMaster. I know you gave permission for your daughter to move into your summer home but her friends are impossible, believe me."

"I did give permission for Fila to move into my summer house, but she didn't say anything about friends," I gasped.

"That's what she told me, Mr. Enderby. Now I don't know what's gotten into young, Ms. Enderby. She was always so reliable and business-like. Now she's spending every waking minute consorting with religious weirdos and those down on their luck. Particularly this fellow," Mrs. McMaster handed me a photograph.

"Religious weirdos," I gasped.

I stared at the photograph in amazement. It was a photo of a young, oriental man with a shaved head wearing thick glasses. He was sitting cross-legged on the floor in my favorite study, dressed in cherry-red and orange robes. The fellow appeared to be in a meditative position. He was chanting in front of my koa desk which had been transformed into some kind of foreign altar complete with statues of Buddhas, incense and floral offerings. Around him, were an assortment of people looking like younger versions of the San Francisco beatniks of the sixties.

"My daughter is having an affair with him?" I gasped, completely shocked. My chest started heaving again.

"Oh, no, not him, Mr. Enderby. That one's just completely taken over your summer home. Thinks he's a direct representative of God, or something. Orders me around in his broken English like he pays my salary. 'Will need refreshments at 7:00, he directs. 'Tirty people coming for poojah, fifteen for Green Taro initiation. Tomorrow, venerable Lama come dinner. Need dining room, setting fo twenty. You take care of, he directs."

"Who do you suspect my daughter is having an affair with, then?" I questioned urgently. I could feel the morphine losing it's effect.

Mrs. McMaster handed me another photograph.

I stared at a picture of a long-haired, bearded fellow in his thirties wearing my favorite blue, silk kimono. Underneath the kimono, he wore my blue polo shirt, my favorite casual slacks and a string of hippie beads around his neck. I choked.

"Whatever makes you think my daughter is having an affair with this man?" I demanded sharply.

"He's living in your master bedroom, Mr. Enderby. And your daughter's moved into the bedroom next to it. Sometimes, she books off work and they disappear into your master bedroom for hours."

"Fila's been booking days off work? When we're having this crisis over that Senior Citizens' lodge she wants razed to the ground."

Mrs. McMaster smiled knowingly. I realized I had to find out what was going on immediately. Pain shot into my lungs. I forced myself to keep from groaning.

"That will be all Mrs. McMaster," I ended the interview.

"But there's more Mr. Enderby," she protested. "Don't you want to hear about the all-night poojah sessions? Or the weekend gatherings they call a retreat. Undesirables come from all over California, I swear."

"I'll get to the bottom of this right away, I assure you, Mrs. McMaster," I tried to appear calm. "Just don't say anything to my daughter or these men and leave me these photographs."

Mrs. McMaster left in a huff.

I opened the desksafe again and injected some more morphine into my veins. Inwardly, I seethed.

None of the promising businessmen I introduce are satisfactory, I cursed. My daughter has to choose someone from another planet.

It must be one of those cults, I gasped as my pain faded. Fila must have been brainwashed. I buzzed my other secretary.

"Janine, have Michael bring my car around to the front immediately."

"But what about your directors' meeting, Mr. Enderby? It's in 15 minutes."

"Cancel it Janine," I directed.

The additional morphine gave me the strength to make it down to my limo. I sank into the back seat with a gasp.

"My summer home at Newport Beach, Michael," I directed my chauffeur and personal butler. "And don't spare the gas."

Michael pulled the limo out into traffic with a vengeance.

CHAPTER 4.

Confrontation.

I removed my mala beads from around my neck as I waited for Fila to appear in the door of her father's master bedroom.

The last few weeks have been so decadent, I said to myself. I certainly got more than I bargained for from the wealthy lady of Orange County.

I'm living in a mansion amongst hand-crafted furniture and priceless art objects. I'm wearing the best of her father's designer clothes, eating gourmet foods and receiving sexual attention on demand, particularly when that test that Fila uses says that she is ovulating. What a contrast to the last 15 years of my life. Since I converted to Buddhism in Nepal, I've been content to alternate between a modest life style when gigs have been plentiful and an ascetic one when gigs have been difficult to attain.

Must be some good karma catching up with me. But I hope I'm not getting accustomed to this luxurious way of life. It has to end once Fila becomes pregnant. After all, one of the main tenants of Buddhism is that life is cyclic. Even good cycles eventually end.

Buddhism does say that all aspects of life and even life itself are impermanent, I reminded myself, but I'm going to miss my uptight, little business lady much more than I anticipated.

I knew that the Buddha instructed his desciples to 'go with the flow' and to avoid either excessive joy at good happenings in life or excessive sadness or anger at bad happenings in life. I tried to return to the customary detachment that it had taken many years of constant striving to accomplish but thoughts of Fila kept entering my mind.

I'm in danger of losing myself to desire, I realised as I thought of Fila's beauty, spirit, and unwillingness to call it quits once she set her mind on something. I realised that one side of her personality had been quite shut down by her father but I found the lady's body and spirit quite attractive. Fila may be driven by her business goals, I acknowledged, but she's the fastest learner of any woman I've taught the secrets of lovemaking. If she'd only let me teach her a little about Buddhist philosophy and tantric practices.

She's too closed, I acknowledged. Too afraid to validate any kind of feeling except that of business accomplishment.

Her father conditioned her well, I reasoned. First she had to earn two degrees in business and commerce and then undergo an apprenticeship with him. All those years of never-ending criticism are a form of abuse. Fila's private life is all but shut down. Her father's trained her to concentrate day and night on achieving the growth of Enderby Development. I imagine that the only way that Fila could get any praise was to succeed in business.

My musing came to an end as the lady herself appeared in the doorway.

Right on time, I noticed. Fila had me scheduled in between her morning business meetings and her noon motivation talks for her sales people. She kept her schedule religiously.

My thoughts turned to more pleasant undertakings as the beautiful lady senuously removed her green, linen business suit in full view of my appreciative eyes and slid under the silk sheets of her father's oversize bed. My body shifted eagerly into full arousal. I massaged areas on her body that I knew warmed the lady up considerably until she was most eager to engage in serious sexual activity.

"My God what's that?" Fila's anguished words jarred my pleasure as she pulled out of my embrace and rushed over to the clothes she had just taken off. She pulled out a portable phone. I came back to the world and realized that the phone had been ringing for some time.

"Forget it sweetheart, it's likely just one of Zot's clients. Those kids seem to need counselling from him day and night."

"Alvin's the only person who has this number, Rolf. It must be important."

"Alvin, whatever is it?" she demanded. "You know I left word at the office not to disturb me. Besides, I thought you just got back from the East Coast."

"Say that again, Alvin." Fila put the receiver next to my ears.

"Your housekeeper blew the whistle on you, darling. The things I go through for you. Why, your father just gave me the third degree trying to pry out what I knew about your love life. And now he's trying to banish me to La Jolla with his pitbull of a secretary, Lucille." Alvin sounded freaked out.

"Alvin, what are you babbling about?" Fila interrupted.

"Got to go. darling. Your father's pitbull is about to return from the loo. She doesn't realize I know how to hotwire this car and that I have this mobile phone."

"Alvin! you're not making sense."

"If I were you, darling, I'd get all traces of whatever is going on in your father's summer house out of sight. I wouldn't put him past him to come flying over there, toodle oo, have to go." The phone went dead.

Suddenly, the sound of a car screeching to a halt in the driveway echoed through the room.

Fila pulled the drapes back far enough back to view what was going on in the driveway.

"My God, Alvin's right, it's my father," Fila screamed. I got up myself and looked through the crack in the drapes. A distinguished looking gentleman was walking rapidly up the driveway. He had a furious scowl on his face.

"Don't answer the door," I advised as Fila hastily flung her business clothes back on.

"That's won't work, Rolf, Father's got a key."

"Damn, Alvin's right, Mrs. McMaster must have told my father about us. I should have foreseen this happening."

"For God's sake put some clothes on," she added. Ones that don't belong to Father. And get Lama Tsot and his students out of the house. I find it difficult to explain him to anyone let alone my father."

I could feel Fila's desperate panic.

"I wonder why this is so important," I thought. I grabbed a robe and tried to remember where I'd left my spartan wardrobe when Zot and I had moved into the mansion on the hill.

The closet, I reminded myself as Fila ran frantically out the door.

"Tell the old buzzard we're engaged," I yelled down the hallway.

"What did you say Rolf?" Fila charged back in the room.

"Pretend we're engaged. Fathers always calm down if you let them think you're going to marry the man they catch you having sex with."

"I never want to marry, Rolf but you're right, that ruse might just work."

"Of course, it will," I said reassuredly. "Here, use this ring." I pulled a small ring off the little finger of my right hand.

"This was my grandmother's engagement ring." Fila quickly placed the ring on her second finger. It fit like a glove.

"This is an exquisite ring, Rolf," she muttered in amazement. The stone was a miniature ruby set in a 24 carrot gold band.

"My grandfather had it styled especially for my grandmother," I explained.

Loud voices came down the hallway from the entrance hall.

"My God, someone's answered the door," Fila gasped. She rushed out again. I realised one of Zot's students had let Fila's father into his house. Fila rushed down the polished wood circular stairway.

The drumming, cymbal clash and Tibetan chanting from Zot's early morning puja session suddenly ceased. Loud voices floated up from the study downstairs.

"What the hell is going on in here?" an older man's voice shouted. "Get out of this house, the lot of you or I'm calling the police to arrest you for trespassing."

"This is Lama Tsot, Father," Fila's agitated voice floated up. "He's a Tibetan Buddhist Lama sent by the Dalai Lama to set up a Dharma Center in Laguna Beach.

These are his students."

"Sure and I'm Santa Claus," Fila's father raged. "You have some major explaining to do, young lady." Mr. Enderby's voice was grim. I heard him tell Fila that he remembered giving permission to her to use his summer home but that she hadn't said anything about boarding religious exotics from foreign countries.

"You heard me," he shouted at the students. "Clear out of here this instance the lot of you." I could hear the shuffle of feet down the hall and the front door slam.

"Tell me one reason why I shouldn't alter my will to set up a private trust to oversee Enderby Developments?" Fila's father yelled.

I threw on the clothes I had been wearing the day I met Fila. I quickly brushed my hair, threw the incriminating bed together and made a dash to the study.

"You have no right to embarrass me like this, father," Fila shouted. "Or to set up a board of trustees over Enderby Developments." I heard her tell Enderby how she had been all but managing it herself lately, quite competently.

"Where is this fellow?" Mr. Enderby demanded, shoving a photograph at Fila. I recognised a photograph of myself as I entered the doorway.

"Mr. Enderby," I put out my hand, "I'm Rolf Nordquist, Fila's fiance." Mr. Enderby turned white as he stared at me. He seemed to choke into the embroidered hankerchief he pulled out of his pocket. Zot was standing in the room, looking dazed. I realised he had to pull himself back from the deep meditation that Lamas entered into when they conducted services.

"You told me to find someone to marry, Father," Fila protested angrily.

"I told you to marry someone capable of managing Enderby Develpments," Fila's father retorted in the coldest voice I had ever heard, "not some leftover draft dodger and drug user from the Vietnam War."

"Rolf no use drugs," Zot protested. "Take oath when become Tibetan Buddhist, not use intoxicants. He no even drink alcohol. Rolf good man, save Lama Tsot's life. Activist fo environment," Zot testified.

"Rolf didn't dodge the draft, father," Fila yelled. "He wasn't old enough. You're making a big mistake. Rolf graduated first in his class from Harvard Business School."

I went into shock. How did the lady know about that? I wondered. She must have had me checked out by a private dick.

"Harvard doesn't train its graduates to dress like that, Fila." Mr. Enderby said sarcastically and stared at my long hair and the mala beads I always wore around my neck with extreme censure. "You should have checked this fellow out before you swallowed his lies."

"I'm a devout Buddhist, Mr. Enderby," I protested, making a great effort to keep my voice calm. "Surely, even businessmen are entitled to their own religious practices."

"Who was the dean of the Business School the year you graduated?" he demanded, his voice full of disbelief.

"Alastair Cross," I replied. "You know, the Alastair Cross that single-handedly started the sub division housing projects that changed the face of California."

"I know who Alastair Cross is, thank you." I realised Mr. Enderby's voice had gone down several decible levels. "But tell me what business projects have you been active in since you graduated? I'm not familiar at all with the name Rolf Nordquist or are you related to the Nordquists in the insurance industry in Baltimore?"

"Rolf active in business in South America," Zot volunteered. "Set up land trusts in Amazon. Not want all Amazon defoliated."

"I've specialized in environmental activism, Mr. Enderby," I said quietly.

"Well, I suppose if indeed you did graduate from Harvard Business School you do represent an improvement over Fila's usual behavior, Nordquist." Enderby told us how Fila usually shied completely away from members of the opposite sex of any background. He said he was beginning to wonder if his daughter was a lesbian? I realised he knew nothing about what motivated his daughter.

"Father, how can you embarrass me like this?" Fila demanded. "Displaying family matters to all the world. And ordering my invited guests out of the door."

"Do you two have a date in mind?" Enderby seemed determined to call our bluff. I realized the old buzzard was hard to fool.

"After the release of my 'Amazon Paradise' CD, Mr. Enderby," I tried to stall. "It's due out in six months at the earliest."

"How about setting the marriage date in three months, Nordquist, at the latest?" Enderby challenged. "My doctor tells me I don't have long to live and I would like to see Fila married before I die."

"Sounds fine to me, Enderby," I bluffed. "What do you think darling?" I referred the matter back to Fila.

"Father, how dare you interfere with my marriage plans. You know I have to settle that Senior Citizen problem before I can do anything else."

"We'll let Nordquist, here, find a way to get you out of that one, Fila. Shouldn't be hard for a Harvard Business graduate, particularly one you seem to think can take over the reins of this business." Enderby's voice was dripping with sarcasm. "A man who graduated at the head of his class."

I couldn't stand the way Enderby was humiliating his daughter.

"You need to do some mediation with those seniors, Enderby," I advised. I told him how there had been too much negative publicity already and that there was no way that City Hall would allow the zoning altered unless the seniors were relocated to somewhere they would feel secure and comfortable.

"Oh, really, Nordquist," Enderby replied, his voice still dripping with venom. "Well, we'll just put you in charge of the mediation, shall we?"

"I'd be delighted to help," I offered.

"You have one month, young woman," Enderby snarled to Fila. "To smooth out the glitches in that Senior Citizen transaction, arrange your marriage plans, and convince me that this so-called fiance of yours has enough business acumen to guide Enderby Developments through the transition of my death. Otherwise I'm altering my will again."

"Lama Tzot help Fila father learn face Bardos before die," Zot volunteered.

"It's an old Buddhist custom," I tried to explain to Enderby who was staring at Zot like he came from outer space. I told him how according to Tibetan Buddhist beliefs, the essence of a living creature was transferred to a place called Bardos after death. I told him that Bardos were somewhat similar to Christian purgatory and that Zot was offering to help him prepare himself for the Bardo experience in advance.

"Most important be calm," Zot advised. "Lose anger, fear dying. May even have chance recognize 'Buddha nature,' escape wheel of life."

"Get out of my house," Enderby shouted at Zot. "Don't try and pull that cult stuff on me. I've heard of con artists like you. I don't require any preparation for death." Enderby pointed out how the brain ceases functioning at death and how you're just gone forever. And that he didn't need any training to cease to exist.

"Get your belongings and get out of my house before I turn you over to the authorities or the Tibetan embassy."

"Lama Zot is a guest in this house, Father," Fila protested. "He's a religious clergyman not a con-artist. I'll not have you treat him like a common criminal." Fila explained how there wasn't a Tibetan embassy and how Tibetans lost their country when China invaded Tibet in 1950.

I was amazed. Fila Enderby was sticking up for Zot. And it appeared that she had actually absorbed some of the knowledge Zot and I had told her about Tibetan problems.

The two Enderby's glared at each other. They remained locked in some kind of mental conflict for well over a minute. Suddenly Enderby lowered his gaze.

"Very well, Fila, if you insist. Lama Zot, or whatever you call him, can remain here. But I'll not have anymore of these confounded religious practices going on in my study. Or my home invaded by members of some weird religious cult."

Enderby's capitulation seemed to throw him into a fit of coughing. I noticed blood on his hankerchief although he tried to hide it.

"I'll find you somewhere else for your center, Lama Tsot," Fila promised.

"And another thing, young lady," Enderby's voice was cold and shaky but rather faint. "I'm moving into this house. I want to keep a close eye on you and your actions. I trust my master bedroom will be ready for me by this afternoon."

Enderby headed for the front door. He left with a bang. The three of us looked at each other in horror.

"What are we going to do now, Fila?" I collapsed on a chair. "My ruse worked but now we're committed to marrying within three months."

"My father won't last three months, Rolf, I promise you'll not have to go through a wedding ceremony. The last thing in the world I plan to do is marry someone, believe me."

"You're probably right about your father, Ms. Helmsley. He's not in very good shape at all. I noticed blood on his hankerchief after that coughing fit."

Privately, I was surprised to find disappointment welling up in my mind. I mentally connected the disappointment to its source. I realised I was somehow disappointed that the last thing Fila appeared to want was to marry me.

My God, I thought to myself. And I thought I had lost all attachment to binding relationships long ago.

"Energy, Mr. Enderby, very bad," Zot agreed. "Tink he may die anytime."

"So Father's moving in, Rolf. That shouldn't alter my plans or our agreement. He can't have long to go."

"What are you going to do about that problem with the Senior's center?" I complained. I felt my energy centers firing up. Somehow the thought of proving myself in business to Fila's father was setting me into a fear reaction.

"The last thing in the world I want to do is engage in business activities," I told Fila. "I gave up that Samaric activity years ago when I converted to Buddhism."

"Samaric activity?" Fila questioned.

I told Fila how most humans were on a treadmill, like a rodent in a cage. I told her how humans die, go to the Bardos not prepared, and that the mind was 10 times as powerful when it was freed from the body. I told her how you must be calm in a bardo, not react emotionally to scary happenings that your mind perceives occurring. I told her that if you panicked, and re-entered a new fetus without enough preparation, you were likely to experience a very disadvantaged re-birth.

"Much bad karma from past lifetimes catch up wit you," Zot added. "Sentient being grow up in west, become conditioned by parents, television, get caught illusions dis world. Dere many traps."

"Yeah, like relationships, career, stardom, sports championships, wealth," I added. I told Fila that the possibilities were almost endless. That, often a person reached the end of their life, entered the Bardos unprepared yet again and then went off on another cyle of disadvantaged existence. I told her that unenlightened existence is called 'Samsara' in Buddhist terminology.

"Mr. Enderby good example," Zot said.

"Live many, many lifetimes," Zot tink. "Still no awareness. He want believe everyting end at death, but not so."

"That's too deep for me, Rolf," Fila said wearily. "It's this life I'm worried about now."

The lady started issuing orders. "Rolf, you had better move your things out of father's bedroom. You can move into the one next to Lama Zot's."

Fila told me that she thought my suggestion for mediation in the Senior Citizen's complex was a good one. She said that one of the city councillors had warned her that it was impossible to get the zoning changes through with the current publicity. She said she would get one of her human resources specialists working on mediation right away. The lady sounded kind of surprised that I could come up with a good business idea.

"And I'll get Alvin to set up some wedding arrangements," she said. "We can both only hope we won't have to go through with them."

"What about Zot's students?" I queried. I wasn't going to let Fila forget about our agreement.

"I'll get one of my rental people on it right away," she promised. "Just keep the students out of here for a while."

"I have phone numbers," Zot assured Fila. "I tell dem wait."

"My God, I'm going to be late for my motivational presentations. Do me a favor, Rolf, will you. Pick up some steaks for me at the supermarket. Father's going to want one for dinner and Mrs. McMaster won't be here till after lunch." Fila handed me one of her credit cards.

"Buy yourself some new clothes, Rolf," she ordered. "We have to make you look more like a potential business executive for father." Fila told me that now I'd have to move into her office at Enderby Developments and pretend that I was coming into the company after our marriage. I freaked.

"I don't want to conduct business, Fila," I protested. "I put that all behind me long ago."

"I'll raise you to twenty thousand a month, Rolf. Just pretend you're calling the shots," she argued. "I'll prep you in advance."

"And pick up a new car for yourself," the lady ordered. "Something more in fashion than that rusted out sedan you drive around. Use the credit card as a down payment. And get a haircut or at least a trim." Fila rushed out the door.

"What have I got us into?" I complained to Zot.

"Haircut no hurt, Rolf," he advised. "Hair grow back. Good karma, help Tsot set up Buddhist center. And remember 'Amazon Paradise' CD."

"You're probably right Zot and my hair will grow back," I answered. "I'll just have to get used to my new look in a mirror." We moved to Enderby's master bedroom to take care of the lady's first command.

"Tsot go grocery store wit you, Rolf? Need some rice fo offerings, Buddhas."

"You haven't been in one of the supermarkets here have you Zot? Sure you're ready for one?"

"Wat you mean, Rolf?"

"You'll see," I promised. Zot helped me move my spartan wardrobe and I drove him over to one of the huge shopping centers. I waited for his reaction as we went into the huge groceteria.

"All dis food, Rolf?" he said in disbelief. "Enuff feed entire village, ten tousand people fo years." I went over to the fish and meat section. Zot gasped.

"So much killing," he sighed. "How many people dis meat fo, Rolf? How meat keep fo such long time witout freeze?"

I told Zot how that meat was just for the immediate neighborhood, and how it would be all gone by the weekend. Zot turned and noticed the Fish section.

"Dat nice, Rolf. Wat you call aquarium, I tink. Nice of store decorate surroundings. Make customers happy."

I told Zot how what he was looking at wasn't an aquarium.

"Wat you mean, Rolf? Oh, no." I ran my index finger across my throat."

"You mean dose fish, crabs, lobsters wait die?" he exclaimed.

"Just like they are on death row, Zot."

"Dat terrible, Rolf. Dey fed anyting? How long dey wait till die?"

"I don't know, Zot. I never thought about that."

"We need chant, Rolf. Bless souls of fish, crabs, lobsters. Dey sentient beings. Need help."

"Later, Zot." I dragged him away from the tanks. "Watch out," one of the store customers ordered as Zot stood in the center of the aisle blocking the way. Zot was staring back at the fish, his eyes wide open in horror.

"Damn you, move," the customer shouted. Zot staggered back as the lady gave him a look that would kill and pushed her shopping cart haughtily by him..

"Crabs even tied up," he said. "And why dey stacked one on top of udder like dat?"

"For freshness, Zot," I replied. "They don't die till they are thrown into a pot of boiling water. That way there is no danger of spoilage."

"Dat awful, Rolf. Dey sentient beings. Dey have feelings just like us. How do you tink dey feel?"

"I never thought about that Zot," I confessed.

I grabbed some of the best quality steaks and moved Zot towards the checkout.

"You drive Zot back beach house Rolf?" he requested sadly.

"You've got tears in your eyes, little buddy," I accused him.

"Want chant fo souls, sentient beings, Rolf. All dese fish, animals dat die here every day, how many die all over west in even one day. Mo dan Tibetans eat in lifetime."

"Watch out you idiot," some fellow shouted at me from his car as I tried to back up. I went back into my parking spot and he shot by driving into a parking space of his own with a squeal of his tires.

"Why, people in west have no patience, Rolf?" he asked.

I realised my little buddy was having one heck of a culture clash reaction.

"They don't call living in a big city in America a 'rat race' for nothing, Zot," I explained.

"Put these into the fridge for me, will you?" I asked as I dropped both Zot and the steaks off. "I have to take care of the lady's other commands."

CHAPTER 5.

One Happy Family.

"Alvin, what do you mean my father is in the midst of moving into his summer house?" I questioned the sanity of Fila's long-time secretary. I went looking for my sister when my father's guard secretary, Janine, wouldn't tell me where he was but she was nowhere to be found either.

"Father never moves to the Newport Beach house until fall when it's a little cooler."

"Really Drew, I'm only telling you what I know. If you don't mind, I've already had enough excitement for today. It took me over two hours to escape from your father's secretary and make my way back to this office. I'm telling you. Both your father and your sister are at the Newport Beach house as far as I know."

"Escaped from father's secretary, whatever do you mean?"

"I'm too tired to explain now, Drew. Just go over to the Newport house. You'll find both your sister and your father there, believe me."

"Alvin, you come with me," I ordered. "I always get lost looking for that house. You'll just have to show me where it is."

"The things I do for this family," he muttered. as I dragged him out. I left the office totally pissed off.

"What are you doing here, anyway, Drew?" Alvin demanded as we went towards my car. "I thought you were out of town for the spring and summer."

I told Alvin that he would have appreciated the last mind-boggling conversation I had with my father when he told me he wanted me back in Orange County immediately. I told Alvin how I was shocked when he said he had been given a death sentence from his doctors and he wanted me back home to learn something about his business before he went.

I filled Alvin in with my end of the conversation, how I'd accused my father of being as healthy as a horse and that I couldn't come back because I had just met this fascinating older woman. I told father that Daphne was a jockey and a horse trainer in Kentucky. I told him how Daphne was a perfect ten, if he discounted height, and how I'd even bought myself several race horses, trying to get to know Daphne better.

I told Alvin how father had cancelled my allowance on the spot. I emphasized father's complete lack of empathy and how he had told me to be in his office within a week after threatening to recall every one of my credit cards. I told Alvin that father had said that he had changed his will to read that inheritance of my Enderby Resources's controlling interest stock, or any stock for that matter, was now contingent upon my marrying and producing a male heir.

"So here I am, Alvin, at pop's office, my new friend Daphne Dugan and her two racehorces in tow," I explained. "After my rent cheque bounced, I realised that my old man was serious. What the hell is going on? I'm sure you know, you always know everything."

"Well, your father does appear to be having a problem with his health, Drew," Alvin said. He told me that it was serious and that Fila had remarked that their father wanted to set things in order before he died. Alvin told me that father had said that he wanted her and I in serious relationships before he died so that he would be sure there would be a grandson to carry on Enderby Developments. His words threw me into a rage.

"Here I am." I exploded, "having driven two race horses through the highway traffic across five state lines to save my budding relationship with the most gorgeous, older woman ever to have mounted a horse, and where is my father? With Fila, just like he always is."

Alvin stared at the horse trailer behind my car and at the woman in the front seat in amazement.

"One thing about you and your family, Drew," Alvin said, "You people are never boring, I'll say that much for you."

I opened the door of my custom-made BMW and sank wearily into the back seat. I motioned Alvin into the front.

"Allow me to introduce my fiancee Daphne Dugan, Alvin. Daphne is a bigwig in horse racing in Kentucky. Daphne, this is Alvin Carstairs, my sister's executive secretary. He's going to drive us over to my father's Newport Beach house. I can never find the place."

"How do you do, Miss Dugan," Alvin reached for Daphne's hand.

"My pleasure, Mr. Carstairs," she replied. "Please call me Daphne."

"I'll bet this car never recovers," I muttered, "after towing that heavy horse trailer across five state lines. I can feel a drop in power already."

"I'm sure your father will be delighted to meet the racehorses, Drew, and your fiancee, Daphne," Alvin said, his voice choked with laughter.

"Tell me Daphne, have you ever been married before?"

"Why, no, Mr. Carstairs," she replied. "Of course, I realize I'm a little beyond the usual age that women marry. But you see, I've devoted my life to my stable. Until Drew came along, that is. He insisted I come back with him to California."

"Really," Alvin remarked. "Please call me Alvin."

"What a drag," I complained to Alvin. He was always so understanding. The two people in the world I would rather never see, my father and my sister, and we have to go visit both of them, I thought. I realised that we might even have to move in with them if I couldn't convince the old buzzard to reinstate my allowance.

"Shouldn't take too long," I reassured Daphne. "I imagine all this stuff about dying must be a crock of shit, but I'll have to find out more any way, just to safeguard my inheritance."

"You promised that your father would be able to relocate my stable and get me established in California in time for the Kentucky Derby," Daphne looked worried.

"Don't worry, sweetie," I reassured her. "The Derby is months away. I'll take care of this matter in less than a week."

Alvin pressed hard on the accelerator and moved out onto the freeway towards Newport Beach.

CHAPTER 6.

Chief Executive Officer Potential.

This can't be Rolf, I refused to believe my eyes as the laid-back, itinerant musician, I had hired for his genetics returned to father's Newport Beach house just before dinner.

He's changed himself into looking like chief executive officer material, I gasped to myself. I stared at the transformed figure in front of me.

Rolf always was gorgeous, I judged, if you didn't mind his casual scruffiness, but now he resembles some youthful Dean of Business at Harvard Business School.

Before my eyes was a beautifully groomed, magnificent specimen of manhood, dressed in a decadently expensive, three-piece business suit. He's had his beard trimmed, and his hair cut and styled by a specialist, I realized. His fingernails look like they've been professionally manicured. Why the only resemblance to Rolf's former self were his Buddhist beads. I think Lama Tsot referred to them as a mala. And the beads are now discreetly displayed over a turtleneck sweater and under the vest of his suit.

"I couldn't have dressed you better myself," I gasped. "I'll have to restrain my female sales people when I take you to the office tomorrow."

"Thank you Fila," Rolf smiled but his expression quickly turned serious.

"I hate to ask but why are there two race horses grazing in the backyard?" Rolf told me how they were devouring father's tropical flower garden and how they were getting dangerously close to being washed out to sea by the waves crashing against father's dock. Rolf claimed that the winds were higher than he had seen them in months and that he had retied father's yacht.

Despite my worries, I had to laugh as I told Rolf that the horses belong to my brother Drew's new love, and that father had ordered Drew to report to Enderby Developments immediately or he would cut off his allowance. I related to Rolf how Drew had arrived on the doorstep around 3:00 p.m., complete with Alvin and an older woman named Daphne Dugan from Kentucky plus two of her race horses. "Seems Drew's latest love interest is a jockey and a horse trainer," I added. "She refused to leave those two horses behind. Insists she's training them for the Kentucky Derby, a likely story."

"You have a very interesting family, Fila. Your father must be livid."

I told Rolf how the race horses and another older woman had sent father into a full-blown rage and then some kind of apoplexy.

"He's lying down now in the master bedroom," I added.

"Aren't there by laws against farm animals in expensive beach front property?"

I relayed how the neighbors had already complained and that Alvin, Drew and Daphne were out finding a racing stable to board the horses as father had ordered. I warned Rolf that dinner would be a bit delayed as Mrs. McMaster had walked out of the door when the horses arrived and that the new housekeeper, maid, and cook sent over by the the employee agency were getting used to the place.

"Michael, father's butler is showing them around," I added.

Rolf broke into a hearty laugh.

"It's not funny, Rolf." I let Rolf know that Drew's presence with a possible future marriage partner meant that we would have to increase the frequency of our lovemaking. I told Rolf that it was imperative that I get pregnant before Drew impregnated Daphne as she was still young enough to have children. To my surprise Rolf wanted more clarification. I wasn't used to employees questioning my orders.

"I don't understand, Fila?" Rolf looked at me for a reasonable explanation. I turned bright red as I was forced to tell Rolf the humiliating truth of my predicament.

"It's not just that I want a baby," I confessed. "Under the terms of father's present will, the controlling shares of Enderby Development's stock go to either Drew or me. They go to first of his children who produces a male heir to the Enderby fortune."

Rolf looked at me in disbelief. He seemed to ponder the situation for a long time in his mind.

"That's ridiculous, Fila," he finally responded. I could feel Rolf's disapproval.

"I know Rolf, but my father won't listen to reason."

"Fila, what happens if you do get pregnant but the child we produce is a girl?"

"We'll have to use ultrasound. If the fetus is a girl, she'll have to be aborted."

"I won't agree to that, Fila. You should have told me what you were after right from the start." Rolf's voice had a funny sound to it.

"I'm a devout Buddhist of Tibetan persuasion, just like Zot." Rolf gave me a lecture about how Buddhists abhor getting involved in ridiculous life crises that cause, at the very least, emotional turmoil and anxiety. He told me how that was what father's demands were creating for Drew and I. Rolf said that aborting a fetus because it was the wrong sex would produce very bad karma for both of us. He said that it was an act that would almost certainly block enlightenment in this lifetime.

The certainty in Rolf's voice shook me. I thought of threatening him or raising the amount of money I was paying him but the look on his face persuaded me against taking either action. I realized that there was no way I could replace him now. The stakes were too high.

"This whole scenario is becoming really bizarre, Fila," Rolf complained. "You and your relatives are totally caught up in Samsara. You need to reconsider what you're doing with your lives.

Believe me, ruthless pursuit of wealth and power never brings happiness in the long run. Just take one look at the mess your father's life has become."

"All right Rolf," I snapped. "Skip the moral lessons." I forced myself to control my anger as I looked at Rolf's body language. The set of his jaw told me I had little room for bargaining. Father had taught me well to detect when threatening or bribing wouldn't succeed in business negotiations. I sensed that Rolf was one step from walking out of the door, Amazon CD, Buddhist center at stake, or not. I decided to try and pacify him.

"You're right, Rolf, we shouldn't use ultrasound," I compromised quickly. I forced myself to make my voice convincing. "I'll just have to take a chance that the child will be a boy. Boys do run in the Enderby line."

I told him how one of my rental people had found a location for Lama Tsot's center, and that it was not far from the house. I offered to pay for the lease for a year in advance and throw in a leased vehicle for Lama Tsot's personal use.

Rolf took a long time to answer. He seemed to go into some kind of meditation for several minutes and then his features relaxed slightly.

"OK, Fila, but believe me, I won't stand for aborting a fetus I've helped create." Rolf's body language was back to normal. "How do we go about increasing our schedule of interaction. Are there any secret meeting places in this house?"

"We'll take advantage of any opportunities, Rolf. Father's yacht is always available for privacy," I told him. "We'll take to doing sunset cruises."

I told Rolf that I had cleared out my office and Alvin's at Enderby Developments and furnished it with a comfortable chesterfield. I told him that I would work out a schedule in between my usual office appointments. I explained that Alvin would understand when he was sent off for frequent coffee breaks.

"OK," he agreed. "But make sure no one gets hold of your computerized appointment schedule," Rolf laughed. "It might be difficult to explain."

"I'll just have Alvin tell anyone that asks that I'm briefing my fiance for an important position in Enderby Developments, Rolf. With your new look you can pass for a budding chief executive officer with flying colors. We'll just keep your office locked. They'll never suspect what we're doing in there."

Rolf smiled.

"God, he's attractive," I noticed. I repressed my feelings as I felt my heart rate increase.

"That you Nordquist?" Father appeared in the doorway. He had a thick file-folder in his hands. Father did a double take as he surveyed the new Rolf.

"May be I have underestimated you, Nordquist?" Father gasped in amazement.

Rolf just shrugged his shoulders.

"I've had a copy of the Elkhorn Senior's Complex file sent over from the office. Every transaction that's gone on is in there. I'll trust you'll familiarize yourself with these contents and report back to me in the office, tomorrow." Father handed the thick envelope to Rolf. Emotion hit me like a ton of brick. Father's words made me feel personally violated. I felt my face turn bright red with humiliation.

"Father, you're removing me from the Elkhorn Seniors' Center deal?" I choked.

"You were in charge Fila." I inwardly cringed as father told me that Rolf and Drew, if he could show him that he was capable of keeping his mind on business, were the most promising hopes for Enderby Developments functioning without a board of trustees in charge. To my horror, father said that my fiancee was going to have to prove he had what it takes to guide his company. And that Rolf had to do that before our marriage in three month's time. He ordered Rolf and Drew to report directly to him as he wanted to know every move that went on.

"Father, I've spent the last two years putting the Elkhorn deal together?" I tried to prevent myself being replaced by my younger, woman-crazy brother and an itinerant musician I had picked up from Laguna Beach. It did no good.

"Enderby Developments can't afford any more negative publicity, Fila. We're becoming the laughing stock of Orange County, and you're being equated with Leona Helmsley."

Rage, sorrow and humiliation flooded my mind. I realized I was on the verge of hysteria. Somehow father's demotion of me made me feel like I was a small child again. It didn't help when Rolf shot me a look saying 'I told you so.' I managed to keep some semblance of control when my brother Drew, Daphne Dugan and Alvin appeared in the room.

"Who's this?" Drew demanded, staring at Rolf.

"This is Fila's fiance, Drew, Rolf Nordquist. Have you found a place for those race horses?" Father answered. Drew did a double take at Father's words. He stared at Rolf and walked around him like a boxer estimating his opponent's strengths.

"We've located an excellent boarding and training center for them just 30 miles out on the freeway, Mr. Enderby." It was Daphne Dugan answering Father's question. "We'll move the horses after dinner. I'm sorry their presence has been a discomfort to you." Daphne stared at Rolf in amazement.

"Don't I know you from somewhere?" she asked.

Rolf put out his hand. "In Memory Of Autumn," Daphne said incomprehensibly.

"Drew's really picked a dilly this time," I thought.

"It's my favorite piece from your last CD," Daphne Dugan added. "I'm one of your most admiring fans, Mr. Nordquist. You're one of my favorite folk singers. I've got every one of the records you've ever put out. But you look different from your album covers, more handsome, if you don't mind me telling you so."

"You're a man of many surprises, Nordquist!" father was looking thoroughly horrified again. A smug look formed on Drew's face.

"You're marrying a folk singer, Fila?" Drew chortled. I turned red. Rolf ignored Drew's remark.

"I'm flattered, Ms?" Rolf laughed, turning to Daphne."

"Dugan," Drew interrupted, jealousy now evident in his voice. "Daphne Dugan. Daphne is my fiancee."

Even more emotion flooded my mind. Fear added it's presence to my rage, humiliation, and sorrow.

So that's how Drew got that woman to move out here with
him, I thought. Rolf and I don't have a moment to lose. I glanced
closely at Daphne Dugan looking for any sign of an expanding
waistline. Nothing was evident.

"Fiancee eh?" Father's eyebrow's rose.

"Tell me, Ms. Dugan, are you still capable of producing offspring?"

Daphne gasped. "I know there's a difference between Drew's
and my age," she replied, "but it's not that great, I assure you."

"I'll take that as a yes to my question," Father announced.
"Rolf and Fila are making marrage arrangements. For three months
from now. Perhaps, they could make arrangements for a double
ceremony?" he challenged.

"Why not?" Drew lived up to Father's challenge.

"So soon?" Daphne Dugan gasped.

"I'm afraid I don't have long to survive in this world, Ms. Dugan.
It would please me no end to see both my offspring suitably married before my demise."

"Oh, I'm sorry Mr. Enderby. It's just that Drew and I haven't
known each other very long. But if that's the case, I guess three
months from now would be fine."

"Alvin, book Daphne in for an appointment," I ordered.

"Certainly, darling," Alvin replied. "I've always wanted to plan
a wedding. We'll do it in honor of the new millennium. Any pa-
rameters, I have to stay within?"

"The wedding arrangements are under your direction, Alvin,"
I ordered.

"Just tell Alvin who you want to invite, Daphne."

"Thanks, Fila." Despite her age, Daphne seemed naive enough
to look grateful.

The front door opened again. It was Lama Tsot.

"Location perfect fo Dharma Center," Zot beamed at Fila. "All Buddha Fields very happy." Alvin, Drew and Daphne did a double take at the Lama's robes and shaven head. Father looked extremely irritated.

"A Tibetan Buddhist Lama," Alvin announced. "Oh, I do like your color scheme. It's so vibrant. You Buddhists have such an appreciation for style."

"This is the Venerable Lama Tsot Rinpoche," I introduced Rolf's strange acquaintance. "He's come from India to set up a Tibetan Buddhist Center at the request of the Dalai Lama."

"Or so he says," Father said. Drew let out a guffaw. "Pleased to meet you, Lama Tsot," Daphne Dugan glared at Drew and put out her hand. "I've studied Buddhism a little myself. From Cambodia. There's a master back home in Kentucky. I took meditation lessons from him, visualization techniques. It's helped me win a number of races."

"So much for scientific knowledge," father said sarcastically.

"You never told me anything about Buddhist meditation lessons," Drew gasped.

"As I've said, we haven't known each other very long, sweetie."

I was impressed by Daphne's calm demeanor.

She's not as stupid as I had her figured out, I realised. That makes her an even greater threat, I decided.

"Tibetan, Cambodian Buddhism principles almost same," Lama Tsot explained. He told us that Cambodian Buddhism was a lesser vehicle, that Cambodian buddhists try to find Nirvana, but think that it would take many lifetimes. That Tibetan Buddhism was a greater vehicle, where it was possible that a person could find enlightenment in may be even one lifetime.

"Dinner is served in the dining room," announced our new maid.

"After dinner," I whispered to Rolf, eyeing my competition. "We'll take the yacht out for a cruise. We haven't a moment to lose."

"Fila, there's almost a hurricane blowing out there," he cautioned.

"Drew," Fathers words shattered my rising spirit. "Report to Fila's office tomorrow. You and Nordquist can share it. I'll have another desk put in. I want your help on that Elkhorn Senior Citizen deal as well as Nordquist's. You'll have to convince me, young man, that you have some business potential if you expect any inheritance from me."

"I'd be glad to, Father," Drew glared at Rolf with great displeasure.

My heart felt like it was shattered.

Now Drew is pretending to take an interest in business, I winced. My worst fears had come true, I mourned. Everything was so simple before father's illness. The Elkhorn deal was to be my crowning glory, I thought. The deal that would convince father that I had what it took to be the chief executive officer of Enderby Developments. And now, I was reduced to looking for wedding chapels while my little brother and my hired musician got to tamper with my projects.

"This whole setup is Samsaric, Fila," Rolf tried to use reason to calm me as we bobbed around on father's yacht in an almost hurricane wind.

"You and your brother are being set up by a fiend," he advised.

"The way out is to refuse to compete with your brother, Fila. Ignore your fear of losing Enderby Developments. Who cares who guides your father's materialistic real estate firm into the next century? Look at all the farmland that's been placed into housing developments in Orange Country. And all the wildlife habitat that's been lost. Do you want to personally contribute to more land desecration?"

Rolf's advice only sent me into a rage. I reached for some of father's aged whiskey to try and calm down.

"Save your energy for sex, Rolf," I ordered. I put father's yacht on it's automatic pilot. "We're far enough out to sea, now. I don't imagine much shipping is out here in this storm. And make sure you report back to me any developments in the Elkhorn project no matter what father orders. I want to know every step that's taking place. I'll do the business thinking for both of us," I ordered.

CHAPTER 7.

Return to Business.

"I swore I would never look at another balance sheet," I complained to Alvin. I forced myself to skim my copy of the Elkhorn Senior Citizens' Complex file in Fila's office.

"I know," Alvin commiserated. "Real estate is so boring. Believe me, if I didn't need the pittance that Fila pays me for all that I do, I'd find something much more interesting to do with my life, too."

"What have I got myself into?" I asked Alvin. I desperately tried to regain balance in my central nervous system. "Your boss and her relatives have completely shattered my normal calm."

"I know," Alvin agreed. "It happens to me here all the time, too."

"Do you know what the terms of the contract I made with Fila demands?" I told Alvin that either I had to go on attempting to bring a child into this world just to satisfy the terms of a demented businessman's will or lose the opportunity to finance a CD that would help guarantee that the Yanomami could go on living their ancient lifestyle.

"Oh, I wonder whose idea that was? My life has been complicated, too, you know," Alvin confided. "Ever since I agreed to come with Fila into her father's business. I should have stayed where I was," he complained.

"What were you before you became Fila's executive secretary?"

"I was Fila's hairdresser," Alvin replied. "She offered me five times my usual monthly income to become her executive secretary. She said she needed someone she could trust. All I could think of is what a wardrobe and lifestyle that would afford. If only I wasn't so devoted to finding my soulmate."

"Even when my father disowned me when I chose Buddhism over his insurance empire, I didn't experience as much anxiety as I am doing right now, Alvin," I confessed. I told Alvin how I had nearly died yesterday when Enderby had asked if I was related to the Nordquists of Baltimore. How all my father needed to know was that the son he still thought was in Nepal was being considered for the chief executive officership of Enderby Developments.

"Oh, he'll probably find out," Alvin replied. "Geoffrey Enderby is diabolical, I know."

We both stopped talking as Drew Enderby suddenly entered the room. He picked up his copy of the Elkhorn file and glared at it.

"So what do all these statements in this damned Elkhorn file mean, Nordquist?" Drew's question pulled me back to the problem on hand. Enderby expected us both in his office in 20 minutes with each of us providing some suggestions for the Elkhorn crisis to show how talented in a business sense we were.

"But you wouldn't know would you? A hick country singer like you couldn't possibly know anything about real estate."

"Oh, and what did you have for breakfast this morning Drew, nails?" Alvin asked.

I smiled at Fila's tall, well-built, good looking brother. I knew better than to let him goad me into an angry response.

"Want to join forces, Drew?" I suggested. "Perhaps, the two of us together can figure out a better way to tackle the Elkhorn project than either of us alone?"

"You kidding? I got this thing all figured out already," he bragged. "Stick to writing music, Nordquist. Or romancing wealthy ladies. You seem to be doing pretty well in the latter area, if you ask me?"

I took a deep breath. Enderby's son seemed to have inherited a talent for insults from his father. I felt my emotions rising. I realised that young Enderby was trying to distract me from concentrating on the Elkhorn task. I ignored Drew and directed my concentration on the business statements in the file.

"Fila's been man-shy for years, Nordquist," Drew tried to bait me further. "Either you're more talented than Don Juan or she's paying you a bundle to get her pregnant. Which is it?"

Despite my resolve I could feel my hackles rising. Fila is right, I realised. She is in a battle with her brother for the controlling interest of this company.

"Tell you what, Nordquist. I'll triple the amount Fila is paying you." I could not believe it as Drew offered to pay me to take a walk right out of his family. Drew offered to even add an allowance for the rest of my life. My blood boiled when he told me that I wouldn't have to make love to his dear sister to earn it.

"How about it or would you rather continue to be a gigolo?" he asked.

Alvin gasped. Rage flowed through me. I got up from my desk and grabbed the young man up to his feet by his shirt.

"Take that back or I'm going to drive you right through the wall," I warned.

"Try it, old man!" he answered. "I dare you."

I started to swing but stopped my fist halfway to his jaw as Alvin grabbed me from behind.

"I don't blame you, Rolf, but remember, Goffrey is waiting for you two," he glared at both us. "In the board room. I'm sure he would find you two covered in blood quite amusing."

"We'll settle this later, Enderby," I managed to gain back some semblance of my rational mind.

"I thought Buddhists were non-violent," Drew laughed in my face. "Perhaps, if I offer you several Buddhist centers for your precious, young Lama? What are you and he, lovers or something? Isn't my sister enough for you?"

I shook with rage as I followed Drew down to his father's office.

You son-of-a-bitch, I thought. You want a battle, you're going to get it.

Enderby motioned us to sit down at the large, polished board room table in his office. Several other business types were already seated. I made sure I wasn't within reaching distance of his son. I wasn't sure I was completely in control of my emotions.

Poor Daphne Dugan, I realised. I wonder if she realises what kind of rattlesnake she's tangling with? I took advantage of the time taken at the start of the meeting as Enderby had his department heads outline the relevant facts of the Elkhorn dilemma. I took a deep breath, managing to calm myself sufficiently to zero in on the Elkhorn profit and loss statements. Something looked irregular to me.

"Well, gentlemen?" Enderby's voice was sarcastic.

"You've all had time to familiarize yourself with my daughter's dilemma. Either we lose an instant 26 million dollars in property gain or we become the laughing stock of Orange County by evicting senior citizens out into the street." Enderby told his business types that the bad publicity the company was receiving was likely to cost it millions in future business.

"What about mediation with the seniors?" I asked.

"It didn't work Nordquist," Enderby snarled. "Those seniors refuse to cooperate. Insist they have a right to stay. Any other suggestions?"

The men around me stared at their Enderby files in embarrassment. I realised that none of them were gutsy enough to challenge Enderby's assessment of the situation.

"Take back the option to purchase Elkhorn, father," Drew spoke out. "Fila's done enough harm to the reputation of this business as it is. The 26 million gain in property value is likely lost anyway."

Anger filled my mind at Drew's public criticism of his sister. I tuned out the voices starting to agree with Drew and mentally sounded a Buddhist mantra to the deity known as Green Tara. From my past experience, I knew Green Tara could be depended on for help in a sticky situation. Suddenly, parts of the balance sheet seemed to lighten up before my eyes.

"What about you, Nordquist?" Enderby's voice suddenly broke through my concentration. "Do you agree with Drew's appraisal of the situation? That we should withdraw our option to purchase?" Fila's old man was forcing me to take a position.

"What would a musician know about real estate?" Drew sneered.

"Removing the option to purchase is going to cost big bucks," I said politely to Drew. "And there is a possible alternative, gentleman, without withdrawing the purchase option." I ignored Drew's insult. A possible solution to the problem had somehow come into my mind as I inspected the profit and loss statements. A whole table of executives stared at me. Drew sent me some energy that caused my throat to choke up. I took a deep breath and mentally chased his energy away.

"You're underestimating the possible earning power of the Seniors complex itself," I told the astonished gathering. I instructed them to take a close look at the recent profit and loss statements for Elkhorn.

Everyone flipped through their Elkhorn files and stared at the profit and loss statements.

"This complex is almost breaking even as it is," I remarked. I pointed out how the revenues were close to covering the expenses, now.

"We can't raise the fees those seniors are paying any more, Nordquist," Drew attacked. He told me in an insulting tone that the seniors were already compensated by the government and that, therefore, those revenues would be frozen for years to come. Drew asked me if I expected Enderby Developments to operate at a loss indefinitely. He told me that no businessman in his right mind would do that.

"But then you're not a businessman, are you?" he accused. "You're one of those bleeding hearts folk singers. I expect you think a wealthy company like Enderby Developments should subsidize those seniors, don't you, something no good business can afford to do for long."

"Businesses should demonstrate some social responsibility," I said calmly. I told the business types that social responsibility and profits were not necessarily incongruent, and that, in this case, they should go for another senior's market.

"Elkhorn property was built years ago right on the ocean before the ocean front became so valuable. Add on another wing to the complex," I advised. I told them how there was sufficient acreage available, and how they should make the new wing one of those, high-rise, new, luxury senior developments that allow individual apartments with back up for extended care. I informed them how that type of unit was being rented and sold for a high price in this country.

"With the well-off, 'baby-boomer,' population in Orange County aging rapidly there's going to be a demand for this type of senior's housing," I ended.

"You're saying that revenues from a new luxury wing of the Senior's Complex would be substantial?" one of Enderby's underlings weighed what I was saying.

"Indeed," I replied. "Enough to justify the construction costs of the new wing."

"That's ridiculous," Drew challenged me. "I say just pull the plug and absorb any losses that result. The losses are income-tax deductible, anyway."

"Stevens," Enderby ordered one of his accountants.

"Draw up a study immediately," Enderby commanded. "Nordquist might have something there. Estimate the cost of construction of a new wing and revenues that would be brought in through sales and rentals. We'll expect your report by Monday at the latest."

"Stevens," Enderby continued. "Notify the press that Enderby Developments is considering taking over the operation of the Seniors' Center itself. To save those senior citizens from re-location, of course. May be that will get some of those bastards off of our back, at least temporarily, until we can figure out what to do."

"This meeting is adjourned to Monday, gentlemen," Enderby emptied the boardroom.

"How could you take the advice of a folksinger over your own son, father?" Fila's brother complained.

"Rolf graduated at the head of his class from Harvard Business School, Drew. Even if he's done nothing since except study Buddhism in Nepal, write music and start up a trust for the Yanomami tribe in the Amazon. I had a look at the detective report Fila had our research department carry out on him."

"The Yanomami tribe in the Amazon," Drew said in disbelief.

Disturbance shot into my heart chakra.

Damn, Enderby knows too much about me, I thought. All he needs to figure out now is that I am related to the Nordquists from Baltimore. All my father needs is an invitation to a wedding from the son he disowned. I thought all of that was behind me.

"That's all Nordquist," Enderby dismissed me. "Drew, I'd like a word with you."

I left the boardroom and returned to Fila's office.

"I don't know how much longer I can go on playing executive for your boss, Alvin," I complained. "I feel like I'm in a pit of vipers."

"I know exactly how you feel, Rolf," he commisserated. "This place has always given me the jitters, too. Everyone is so serious around here, almost like they are obsessed if you ask me."

I was surprised when Alvin gave me some advice. He told me what he did when he felt like bolting. He said that he went and talked to someone who he knew had his best interests at heart.

"In my case it's my beautician, Ariel, he said. "In your case, why don't you go talk to that young Lama of yours. Lama Tsot, isn't it? I'm sure he has your best interests at heart."

"You know that's not a bad idea, Alvin," I replied. "I can see why you're indispensible to Fila."

"I'll go with you Rolf. I don't want to be in this office with Fila and Drew together. You can't imagine how the two of them carry on. Talk about sibling rivalry."

Alvin and I left Enderby Developments office and headed out for Zot's new Dharma Center in the luxurious sedan Fila had provided for me.

I need to talk to a Lama, fast, I told myself. Even if he is 25-years-old and recently from Tibet.

I hadn't felt like murdering someone for years.

All my training to remain calm under all circumstances is being undermined, I realized with panic. That young man and his father are bringing out the killer instincts in me. We must have been adversaries in a past lifetime or something. I felt completely unsettled.

CHAPTER 8.

Tibetan Buddhism
Comes To Orange County.

I reached the immense shopping center that Fila had chosen for Zot's center in less than an hour. My foot had floored the accelerator on the sedan. I realised that anger and anxiety were doing a good job of chipping away at the calm mindfulness I had taken 20 years to develop.

"How did Fila ever get permission from the shopping center to set up a Buddhist center here, Rolf?"

"It's because of the Evangelical church that's already here, Alvin. One of Fila's retail people threatened the management of the shopping center with charges of religious discrimination if they didn't agree to the lease."

"What a concept," Alvin replied. "Religious shopping. Imagine. You get a choice of two religions, under one roof. But I wonder if the residents of Orange County are ready for Tibetan Buddhism. People here are generally very wealthy, you know, and very conservative."

"I know," I replied. "I think Zot would have done better to have tried Los Angeles."

"Oh my," Alvin announced as we walked into Zot's center. "Whatever is that fellow doing?"

I smiled as I glanced at one of Zot's loyal students dangling from ropes from the ceiling. He had an electric sanding machine in his hand and was attacking the top of a tall, cement slab that had been hastily poured.

"Oh, that fellow is shaping a Buddha head, Alvin," I advised. "This is the shrine room, I imagine."

"Well, they'll have a hard time getting that out of here," he laughed "if this center doesn't last. That Buddha is going to be over 12 feet high."

"I like those," Alvin pronounced, looking at the paintings students were hanging on the walls. "What scenes!"

"Oh, those are Tankha paintings, Alvin. Scenes that depict Buddhist history. All Tibetan shrine rooms have them."

"How cross-cultural," Alvin remarked. "What's going on over there?"

I glanced in another corner. A group of three students were seated around a table copying Tibetan chants and their English phonetic translations onto sheets of paper to be laminated.

"Those are for the Buddhist services, Alvin. They're reproductions of ancient Tibetan chants."

"Awesome, I'm sure."

"Where's Lama Tsot?" I asked one of the students.

"He's in his office," the young, blonde fellow answered. "Counselling some client." He pointed over to a small room that had already been roughed out with gyproc. It was out of all the building activity.

I walked over to the back room. It's door was closed. We sat down on chairs and waited for the office's occupants to emerge. I fell into deep meditation trying to still the anxiety and fears my involvement with Fila and her family were raising. I came back to consciousness with a start as a woman came out of the office with Zot. I shook my head in surprise as I realized it was Daphne Dugan, Drew's fiancee.

"Why, it's Alvin and Rolf," she beamed.

"So nice to see you. Won't you join us?" she invited. "Lama Tsot is coming with me to bless my new training stable. It's less than an hour from here via the freeway."

"But of course," Alvin agreed. "What a blast." Zot came out of his office. He had gathered up a number of objects for the blessing in a duffle bag.

"Rolf, wat you do here?" he asked.

"I need some counselling, little buddy, but it can wait until you get Daphne's stable and her race horses blessed, I guess. Come on, I'll drive us over to the stables."

My spirits rose as I drove Fila's high powered sedan down the freeway. I left my worry about my involvement with Fila behind me as I stopped my anticipation of future doom and gloom. Alvin, Zot and Daphne were engaging in friendly banter and their mood seemed contagious. I noticed how deep blue the sky was and the intensity of the multi-colored gardens surrounding the residences and office complexes that could be glimpsed from the freeway.

"I'm even forgetting to smell the roses," I told myself as I realised how much I was starting to anticipate some kind of disaster happening as a result of accepting Fila's offer.

Within an hour I was driving up a lane into some of the last remaining farm land areas in Orange County. Despite the productivity of the land and the availability of cheap labor from across the border, residential sub divisions, high tech business complexes and an endless array of shopping centers were gradually eating up any open space in the County.

"It's that stable, there, Rolf," Daphne directed me.

I whistled as I got out of the car.

Daphne's new training stable is state-of-the-art, I mused. Why, there must be room for over 20 race horses. And there's even an exercise paddock and a track the size of a normal racetrack. Daphne's two horses look lonely, I decided as a stable-boy led them around the huge exercise paddock on long ropes.

"How did you and Drew find this place so quickly, Daphne?" I asked.

"Oh, we didn't Rolf. We just found a place to board the horses that first night. It's all because of Geoffrey Enderby. He's so understanding," Daphne confided.

Daphne told us how Enderby had reinstated Drew's allowance and how he had one of his employees find the new stable complex. Daphne said that Enderby had purchased the place for

Drew and herself as a marriage present. Drew's fiancee said that she had advised Enderby that she didn't need anything even nearly as elaborate but that he said that he wanted to enlarge the stables and purchase at least another 10 race horses with good lines for her and Drew.

"Geoffrey says that I should take part in the race course not far from here at Del Mar, Daphne added. "That he would buy us a membership in the Del Mar Thoroughbred Club."

Excitement formed in Daphne's voice as she told me how she wanted to concentrate on her two, three-year-old horses she had brought from Kentucky.

"I'm convinced that one of them will come in the top three at the Kentucky Derby if only I can finish their training on time," she confided.

"If you want my advice, darling, take advantage of Geoffrey's offer," Alvin advised. "You've got him at a disadvantage right now. He's desperate to get Drew tied down in a suitable marriage."

"Do you know why Drew is so estranged from his father, Alvin?"

"Just make sure when the pre-nuptial agreement for the wedding is drawn up that you list your two horses as your assets, darling," Alvin advised Daphne.

"You think that's necessary, Alvin?" Daphne said in surprise. "Why, Rainbow's End and Gypsy Strolling are like my own children. I've raised them from colts. They'll do anything for me. I wouldn't want to lose those horses for anything."

"Take advantage of the pre-nuptial agreement that will be drawn up," Alvin advised, "and don't use the horses as collateral for any debt on this operation."

"May be you're right, Alvin. Geoffrey's putting this racing stable into Drew's name."

"You've got to watch out for California's community property laws. I'm sure, there's no reason to doubt that your marriage will last forever but if you feel that strongly about the horses follow my advice."

Zot got out some implements from his duffle bag and started chanting in Tibetan. We followed him from place to place as he blessed both the horses and their surroundings with burning incense and sprinkles of water. The ceremony lasted for over 20 minutes. Alvin looked on in amazement.

"How extraodinary," Alvin commented. "I'm always so impressed with rituals."

"Thanks very much, Lama Tsot," Daphne pressed several bills into Zot's hands. "Now I can't lose at the Derby for sure."

I drove all of us back to the shopping center and Daphne directed me to where her car was parked.

I waved her off and Alvin and I followed Zot back to his office.

"Do you mind if I study Lama Tsot's counselling technique?" Alvin asked. "I get to do so much of that myself. I'm always looking for counselling tips."

"Not at all, Alvin," I remarked. "Feel free to join right in."

"Wat problem, Rolf?" Zot asked as I sat down rather dejectedly in his office.

"I'm really worried, Zot," I confessed. I told him how Geoffrey Enderby had managed to get his daughter and son locked into some kind of total warfare over the resources of Enderby Developments. I complained about being right in the middle of it, and told Zot that Fila had gotten herself and me entered into some kind of competition with Drew and Daphne to see which of us could produce a baby boy in record time.

"Not to mention this marriage I'm supposed to go through," I added. "It's getting too close too fast."

Zot nodded.

"We do 'Phowa' Rolf," he ordered. "Transfer consciousness to Buddha fields."

Zot, Alvin, and I moved over to the small shrine he had set up in his office. Alvin and I sat on one of the meditative cushions on the floor in front of the shrine. Zot sat down by his ancient meditation instruments he had brought from Tibet and started to chant in Tibetan.

"Groovy," remarked Alvin.

I removed my mala from around my neck and joined Zot in the ancient chants and mantras I had learned studying in caves overlooking the Himalayas long ago. Before long my consciousness seemed to go elsewhere. I awoke when Zot sounded the cymbal that signalled the end of the 'Phowa' session.

Zot slowly opened his eyes and turned to me looking serious.

"Rolf, important fo you have mo compassion. Buddhas say must try have mo understanding. Boss Enderby Developments ill, very sick. He losing everyting. First wife, now health, life, business, family, homes, plans fo future. Soon he go on to Bardos. Must leave all behind. Natural fo him be angry, try make plans fo his business carry on."

"I gave up on taking part in modern business and commerce long ago, Zot," I complained. I told him and Alvin that I had vowed that I would never have anything to do with materialistic wasting of the earth and its resources, including people, ever again.

"Are you sure I should continue to take part in Fila's mad scheme to gain ownership of her father's company?" I asked. "This whole scenario is getting too bizarre, even for me."

"Buddhas say dis center important, Rolf. You know situation in Dharamsala." He told Alvin how a tiny place in India was supporting all the children and adults that had escaped from the Chinese invasion of their country. Zot claimed that the Chinese government would not let the Dalai Lama back to Tibet unless he become a puppet for them, and that it was possible that Tibetan refugees, children, monks, and lamas would never get to go home.

"Wat Dalai Lama to do?" he asked. "Must locate Tibetan Buddhist Centers in west. Else Tibetan culture, religion, lost foever."

"How dreadful," Alvin remarked.

"I know, Zot. I can't bear to think that the high spirituality I came into contact with over 20 years ago will just be extinguished and the Tibetan people doomed to wander the earth, homeless and cultureless, forever. But do we have to set up a center here in Orange County? Surely, there must be some other place."

"Zot tink people in Orange County need ancient Buddhist teachings. All dey know, materiality. My students tink life here in west last forever. Dat people stay young forever. Dat all matter career, relationships, new homes, babies. Tibetans know dat not so."

"Oh, that's the effect of Hollywood, Lama Tsot," Alvin interrupted. "If you watch closely you hardly ever see anyone over 30 on the tube. And once the characters on television solve their relationship problems, always heterosexual of course, they live happily ever after."

"Land trust in Amazon you set up, important, too, Zot continued. "Yanomami one of last ancient world cultures. Zot tink Rolf have carry on agreement with Fila Enderby. Tink good karma outweigh bad karma."

"What about any offspring I might produce with Fila, Zot? She's trying her best to get pregnant, believe me."

"You be good father, Rolf. not worry."

Alvin broke into laughter at my expression of horror.

"Good God," I shouted. "Zot, the last thing in this world I want to do is bring a child into this materialistic world, or be a husband and father. All I want to do is go back to my old way of life."

"Dis good practice fo you, Rolf, " Zot assured me. "May be Rolf getting stuck in rut dis life. May be dere mo to life dan music, Buddhist philosophy and Yanomami. You have opportunity fix Enderby Developments."

"Good luck," Alvin offered. "I've been doing my best at that for years and haven't even made a dent."

Zot smiled at the frantic look on my face.

"Dis like 'Chod' practice, you do in Nepal, Rolf. Remember, Master Rinpoche have you practice meditation in graveyard late at night. Learn overcome fear. Be ready Bardos when die."

"What a concept," Alvin remarked, "overcoming fear rather than running from it."

I thought about what Zot was saying. 'Chod' practice had been very difficult for me. I remembered the vivid hallucinations I'd experienced in my younger years as I'd spent night after night doing solitary meditation in one of the open spaces in Nepal where dead bodies were carved up for the vultures.

"Must concentrate on wat called 'ground luminosity,' blue sky, not clouds that obscure, or on ocean, not waves dat rise in it, Rolf," Zot did his best to get me to understand. He told me that I was concentrating lately on clouds and waves, and that these were not permanent, that they changed minute by minute.

"Only 'ground luminosity' permanent, Rolf," he added. "Buddhist realise true nature of mind, reach enlightenment even dis lifetime. Only ting really permanent."

I knew what Zot was trying to tell me. Tibetan Buddhists were taught not to consider things of this world as being permanent, and not to consider the circumstances of life to be real in a true sense. All were fabrications, creations of the mind. Death can come for a sentient being at any moment. Possessions can be destroyed at any time. Relationships end all too suddenly for one reason or another. The beloved family dog can suddenly get hit by a car. Zot was telling me that I needed to flow more with the Enderby Developments situation. That whatever was happening that seemed so threatening was only temporary in the long run.

"Also important!" Zot's voice got very serious. "Rolf must face fear business accomplishment. Fixing Enderby Developments 'Chod' practice fo you. Must learn not run when someting treaten."

Zot's words scored deeply. I realized what Zot was saying was affecting me intensely. Suddenly all three of my lower energy chakras fired up, particularly the stomache center. I felt like I had indigestion from red hot chili. I started doubling over in pain.

My God, Zot is already a master teacher, I thought. At his age. He's causing me to confront something I've refused to come to grips with in this lifetime. This latest crisis is not just about Fila and her father.

Why, I've always prided myself for giving up wealth and the family business to become a folk singer. May be there's more to that decision that I thought. Suddenly, I sensed that there was a lot of left-over business connected to my career choice of long ago. I felt Zot sending energy at me. I sensed I hadn't been willing to confront my situation thoroughly, years ago, even when I studied under a Buddhist master in Nepal. Zot's words were plunging me into the grip of a major growth period.

"You're going to be a great teacher, little buddy," I confessed to Zot as I started to confront the enormity of the unfinished business from my youth I had yet to deal with.

"All that running from my father, I did, Zot," I confessed. "All that eagerness to flee to Nepal rather than prove my worth to him in his own field." I felt myself being overcome with emotion.

"Enuff fo now, Rolf," Zot cautioned. "We end meditation session."

I closed my eyes as Zot chanted the customary Tibetan dedication of the session for the benefit of all sentient beings.

"I'll try to be nicer to Enderby, Zot," I promised as the dedication ended. I could feel some of my own pain being lifted as well as that of others. "And to Fila and Drew."

I can see that their father is a lot like my father, I thought. Constantly watching to see if his offspring were going to measure up to super-human business demands. No wonder Drew escaped into pursuing older women. Fila didn't escape. She's been trying since her teens to match up to Enderby's expectations. Only, it's even worse for Fila. Somehow she got mixed up on his goal for her. She thought he wanted her to replace him and all he wanted was for her to marry Mr. Super-Businessman.

I escaped into folk music and the religion of a foreign land. I could hardly have found anything that would have shocked my father more. I can see why this situation bothers me so much, I thought. Fila and Drew's situation is so much like my own past. No wonder, I'm being triggered today by Enderby throwing tasks at me to see if I'm the answer to his business leadership succession problem. Because I ran from the same situation with my own father.

"Best you try mo compassion, Rolf," Zot ordered.

My head reeled. More compassion for Enderby. I might as well try and find more compassion for my own father?

"That's asking a lot, Zot." I found myself fighting Zot's advice.

This must be a 'Chod' lesson, all right, I muttered. I always found them the hardest to learn.

I found myself reeling as Alvin and I left my not so little buddy to get on with setting up his center.

"These kids don't know what they are in for," I said to Alvin as I made my way through Zot's young students.

"They think he's going to help them solve their relationship difficulties or teach them to find Nirvana and instead they are going to have to face what it really is that they came on this earth to do."

CHAPTER 9.

A Replacement For Enderby.

I can't believe that my prayers have been answered, I felt gratitude replace some of my customary anger as I injected a large quantity of morphine directly into my thigh. The veins in my forearms were now refusing to accept the larger and larger quantities I was forced to inject to carry myself through each day. I realised that I had nearly had it. That my days were truly running out. Fatigue followed me every waking moment.

At least some of my prayers have been answered, I mused as the drug did it's job. Drew's not showing much business management potential but at least he's stopped chasing every older woman he meets around Orange County. Thank God for Daphne. And all she required was a small investment in a racing stable.

At last, I might have something positive to say to Fila. I did a last minute cover-up of the myriads of lines that had developed lately in my face. My daughter was due for an appointment in five minutes. I could hardly hold my excitement about what I might be able to tell her if she answered the question I had to ask her with what I wanted to hear.

The buzzer went off on my desk.

"Ms. Enderby is here to see you, sir." I placed my morphine supplies back in my desksafe and released the button that unlocked my office door.

Fila came in looking apprehensive.

Despite how elated I felt, I stayed behind my desk instead of rising to my feet. I didn't want Fila to get a close-up of my face. The make up was only working now from at least two feet away.

"Well Father," she questioned, anxiety in her voice.

"There's something I have to ask you Fila. And I want you to answer honestly. It's of the utmost importance."

"What is it, Father?"

"Whose idea was it to add a wing to the Elkhorn Senior Citizens' Complex, your's or your fiance's?"

"What are you talking about father?" Fila's voice told me what I wanted to hear. She obviously didn't have a clue what I was talking about.

"We should just go ahead and bulldoze that Elkhorn property," Fila continued. "You told me never to cave in to the demands of activists and whackos."

"Rolf has found a way to rescue the Elkhorn project, Fila," I could hardly keep my elation out of my voice. "Didn't he tell you about it?"

"I've been busy touring wedding chapels for three weeks, father, like you told me to. I've hardly even seen Rolf, you've been keeping him so busy. As far as I know he's still weighed down by going over all those files you sent over to the house with Alvin. What do you mean, he's found a way to rescue my project?"

I ignored Fila's look of fury.

"I've been evaluating Rolf, Fila, thoroughly. I had to find out what he was made of." I told Fila that I was very pleased that she had found a man to marry that was worthy of Enderby Developments. I mentioned to Fila how Rolf was able intuitively, to evaluate every one of the projects that we were currently working on or even thinking of undertaking, and how I had looked at the studies prepared by accounting and estimates based on recommendations Rolf had made for her Elkhorn project. I told Fila that Rolf was absolutely right that Elkhorn would pay it's own way and result in a future bonanza if another wing was added to the complex.

"Pour more money into that run-down Seniors' Center!" Fila objected.

"To build a wing composed of luxury condominium residences connected to the latest in advanced geriatric care, dear. Rolf is right. Those units are selling like hotcakes, there's such an increase in the elderly population. And many of them are quite wealthy."

Fila looked like she was trying to process what I was saying.

"I want you to instruct Alvin to speed up your and Drew's marriage plans, Fila," I ordered. I told her that my doctors had warned me that I was not going to last three months, and that I could tell I wasn't going to have the strength to attend to business much longer."

"I'm going to have to name someone to lead this company through my transition," I added. "I'm going to name Rolf as acting chief executive officer. I want you two married when I make the announcement."

"You're going to make Rolf the acting chief executive officer, Father?" I noticed Fila's voice was choked with emotion.

"At last I've done something to make her happy," I sighed.

"Yes, and I'll leave my present will intact instead of setting up a private trust. Rolf can oversee the business until my grandson from either you or Drew is old enough to take command."

Fila dabbed her eyes. She seemed to be fighting back heavy emotion.

"Fila," I tried to be let her know how pleased I was that she had found Rolf. "I've been evaluating executive potential for years. Believe me, Rolf is a natural. It's the way he interacts with staff and can instantly size up situations. He has an unusual calm and self-confident approach."

"Now go and take care of moving up those wedding plans," I ordered. "I want to see both my children married within one month."

"Father, it's going to be difficult for Alvin to finalize those wedding plans that quickly." Fila's voice was full of emotion.

She must be pleased that she's finally managed to do what I've always hoped for her, I decided. Attract a world-class businessman to guide Enderby Development for the new millennium.

"Tell Alvin that money is no object, Fila, Time is more important." I dismissed her. I could feel the burning sensation that signalled the start of a major coughing fit. I managed a few more words. I had so much to say to my daughter now that she had finally lived up to the life goal I had set for her.

I told her that now that she had finally located someone with the potential to guide Enderby Developments I was going to leave my present will intact.

"Now if only you and Rolf can have a son," I added, "you'll meet the conditions of the will to inherit the controlling stock of Enderby Developments. And even if Drew and Daphne have a son before you, Rolf can guide the company until my grandson is old enough to take over. Now I can die with a certain amount of peace."

Fila rushed out the door.

"Speed up those wedding preparations," I told her before the door closed.

CHAPTER 10.

Upping The Ante.

I noticed right away that my boss didn't have her usual self-confidence. She was sitting behind her desk in our office with a glass of her father's favorite whiskey in her hand.

I took a closer look at the lady's face. Fila's usual state-of-the-art make up was badly messed up. Mascara had spread itself onto her cheeks and her white polyester blazer had dark marks on it. I realized that Fila had been crying profusely.

"Darling, whatever is the matter?" I asked. "You look like a disaster." I told her that Rolf or her brother would be there any minute and reminded her that it was important to look devastating.

"Alvin, we have to talk," she replied. I detected quite a slur in her voice. I was shocked as Fila seldom drank more than one whiskey at any time.

"What is it, darling?" I joked. "I've never seen you so distraught."

"It's a disaster, Alvin. Your plan to make me interim CEO has backfired. Rolf's so impressed my father that he's going to name him as interim chief executive officer instead of me."

"Well, I advised you to find someone to produce a baby, darling. I never said anything about bringing them to the office," I protested. "That was your father's idea if I remember correctly."

"And father wants you to move the wedding arrangements up to the start of next month, Alvin." Fila told me that her father's doctors said that he didn't have much longer to live. Fila complained that she never wanted to marry anyone and that she couldn't imagine Rolf going through a marriage ceremony.

"The start of next month," I exclaimed. "That's only three weeks away."

"I know, Alvin. What are we going to do?"

The door suddenly opened. Rolf came into the room.

"You're on your own, darling," I advised. "Try a little honesty for a change." Fila looked at me in horror.

"Try a little honesty for a change?" Rolf echoed. "Whatever for?"

"I'm going to have to throw myself on your mercy, Rolf," the lady apparently decided to follow my advice. "Something I've never had to do before with any man."

"Must be pretty important," Rolf laughed.

"Rolf, Father wants the date of our marriage moved up to the start of next month," Fila explained. "What will it take to get you to go through that marriage ceremony with me?"

"Hey, that wasn't the deal, Ms. Helmsley," Rolf protested. "Remember, you assured me that your father would have passed away by the time the wedding day came up."

"Father's outfoxed us, Rolf," Fila explained. She told him that it was all because of him because he had followed her directions only too well. Fila told him that he had so impressed her father that he wanted to name him as the interim chief executive officer of Enderby Developments instead of her, until either Drew or her had a son old enough to take over.

"Father wants us married when he makes the announcement and his doctors are adamant that he doesn't have three months to live," Fila added.

"Fila, you know it's nothing personal," Rolf said, "but all I want to do is go back to my old way of life. You Enderbys don't realize it but there are people who don't enjoy the adrenaline surge of your way of doing business."

"I can certainly testify to that, darling," I added.

I listened to their interchange. It was like watching a ping pong game. They shouted at each other back and forth. I wasn't sure either one of them was hearing what the other was saying.

"You'll be able to return to your old ways, Rolf," Fila promised. "Only just go through the wedding ceremony with me." She explained that he was going to stay in her employ until she got pregnant anyway, and that this way she could hopefully avoid Drew interfering in the business operations of the company as that would be totally disastrous.

"What will happen when your father dies, Fila?" Rolf replied. "I have no wish to drag this pretense on past the time my new CD comes out."

"May be I'll be pregnant myself by then, Rolf. I can only hope so. Drew can't inherit the controlling shares and hope to participate in management decisions unless he has a son before I do."

"This whole situation is absurd, Fila. Surely, your father would be better to set up a private trust than rely on me. I'm beginning to feel like 'the great imposter,' or something. And you and your brother are being manipulated by a fiend."

"Hear, hear I can testify to that," I reinforced Rolf's point.

"Look Rolf," Fila bargained. "I just need more time to figure out the best way to proceed." Fila offered to double his salary and pay for Lama Zot's lease for three years in advance. She even offered to make a $50,000 donation to his land trust in the Amazon. All she asked in return was for him to go through the ceremony and keep up the pretense for a little longer.

"That would mean that I'll have to take command of Enderby Developments, Fila," he replied. "At least until your father passes away."

"I'll make the decisions for you, Rolf. Just ask me before you go ahead and solve everything on your own. That's what's got us into this mess."

I remembered Lama Tsot's advice to Rolf. "Rolf need fight business aversion," he'd said.

I interrupted the discussion again.

"Remember Lama Tsot's advice, Rolf. He said to do a little 'Chod' training, I think that's what it's called." I told him that doing so would allow Lama Tsot to establish Tibetan Buddhism more thoroughly in Orange County. I reminded Rolf of the Dalai Lama's dilemma, and how he was now the leader of a huge group of child and adult refugees without a land base to support them.

"And what about all the adherants of his high spiritual, 2500-year-old religion?" I goaded, "are you going to sell them short? Just because you are afraid of business accomplishment."

I could see Rolf's resolve weaken.

"How long will the Dalai Lama even be welcome in Dharamsala?" I added. "What difference would a little more pretense make, any way? "Perhaps you could even guide Enderby Developments into more social responsibility on it's projects, that would be a first."

Rolf looked at Fila.

"You'll go along with my suggestions on the Elkhorn project?" he asked. "And you'll continue to fast track that new geriatric wing?"

Fila turned white. But she nodded.

"And you'll try to develop more social responsibility when your business needs clash with social needs?" Rolf demanded.

"Don't push it Rolf."

I smiled. My boss was sounding a little more like her normal self.

A knock sounded on the door. "Ms. Enderby, your father is looking for you and Mr. Nordquist." It was Lucille, Enderby's secretary.

"He wants to speak with you both in his office."

"Thank you, Lucille, tell him we'll be right there," Fila answered.

"Well, what about it, Rolf?" she asked. "I'll meet all your demands, even the last one." Fila's eyes were begging Rolf to help her out.

"OK, Ms. Helmsley," I sighed in relief as Rolf gave in. "But for God's sake use a justice of the peace for the wedding ceremony,

Alvin," Rolf directed. "I don't want to go through some binding vow I won't be able to free myself from in the future."

"And I'm only going to play CEO until my latest CD comes out at the latest," he warned. "I'm going to have to personally promote it for the disc to impact."

"Thanks Rolf," Fila gasped.

"I'll arrange the justice of the peace," I promised.

The lady managed a wan smile. "That gives me another five months. Surely that will be time enough."

My boss freshened up in the loo. Then we all went down to Geoffrey's office. Drew and Daphne were already in the room with Geoffrey. I could tell Drew was not a happy camper by the look of death he gave Rolf.

"Has Fila told you the news, Rolf?" Geoffrey sounded almost jovial as he, Fila and I sat down in the crowded office.

"You want me to take over as interim chief executive officer of Enderby Developments, Sir?" Rolf answered. I could see Drew flinch in the corner.

"Call me Geoffrey, Rolf," he asked. Drew flinched again.

"Yes, in three weeks, after the wedding, if you can keep showing me you have the unusually astute business mind I'm positive now that you have."

I glanced at Drew and I could see his fingers whiten around the wine glass that Enderby had handed him.

"A toast then," Geoffrey poured some of his expensive sherry into our glasses.

"To Rolf and Fila," he pronounced. "The two of you are going to lead Enderby Developments in the new millennium."

"What about me, Father?" Drew demanded. He had hatred and jealousy written all over his face. "You'll have to be the first of my children to produce a son, Drew. If you want more than the vice-presidency of the company. I only hope you can learn some business sense from Rolf. God knows I haven't been able to instill it into you."

I gasped at Geoffrey's outspoken comments. Somehow Rolf was going to try and co-exist with a brother-in-law who hated his guts.

My, this situation gets more interesting all the time, I thought. I haven't been this amused at anything that's happened at Enderby Developments since I came here.

"I want you back at the office after dinner, Rolf," Geoffrey commanded. He told Rolf that he had to fill him in on the details of all the irons Enderby Developments has in the fire. He asked me to come along as well as he needed me to pull some files from the records. He told Rolf and I that there was myriads of work to do."

"Sure Geoffrey," Rolf answered. I tried not to enjoy the look of pure hatred Drew threw at him.

That puppy is getting his just deserts, I thought. Geoffrey should have taught him to heel years ago.

I drove Geoffrey and Rolf back to the offices at 7:00. By midnight I could tell Rolf was in excruciating pain.

"All my chakras are lit up and my anxiety level is at an all-time high," he confided when Geoffrey left the room for a minute.

"I had no idea Enderby Developments had so many projects involving the military," he complained to me. "And all these projects are going on simultaneously." Rolf said that Geoffrey's had 15 projects in Orange County under construction alone. And that his out-of-state investments must be in the multi-millions. Rolf asked how Geoffrey even managed to be aware of what's happening everywhere?

"Delegation is Geoffrey's secret, Rolf," I confided. I told Rolf how Geoffrey had Fila supervising most of the projects in Orange County, and how he recruited the best of the graduates from key university business centers for the out-of-state scene.

"Geoffrey has them competing with each other to move up the upward mobility ladder," I advised.

Geoffrey's voice was full of fatigue when he returned.

"These late sessions aren't good for your health, Geoffrey," I warned.

"My health is shot, Alvin. I'm a goner for sure. There's no way I can beat this disease back. God knows I've tried." Geoffrey told us that he was so pleased that Fila had gone and done what he'd been wanting her to do for years, to find a replacement for himself. He told Rolf that he was showing more promise than any of his old and reliable executives, and that he was outshining even his most promising recent graduates. He told Rolf that he liked his way of evaluating both his projects and his staff.

"You've got a real knack for getting to the nuts and bolts of something immediately," he added.

"Thanks, Geoffrey. I think," Rolf replied. Geoffrey reached for more files. I glanced at them and realised Geoffrey was concentrating on the Orange County projects.

"Shouldn't Fila be part of this discussion, Geoffrey?" I asked.

"To be honest," he replied. "I want Rolf to evaluate these projects on his own. I've had misgivings about the way Fila tackles things for some time." Geoffrey confided to Rolf that Fila was too quick to try and dominate a project. He said that it was almost like she was competing with his top management people all the time. Geoffrey complained that he didn't know what had gotten into his daughter. He said that Fila shown a lot of promise when he first made her a vice-president but that since his illness she had been much too aggressive, and too quick to fly into something without proper thought.

"Why don't you get a little rest, Geoffrey?" Rolf suggested. "I'll go through these files with Alvin and we can discuss them tomorrow."

"OK, Rolf," he agreed. "Take these files into your office, will you? I'll get some rest on my couch for the night. I'll expect you at seven in my office."

I crept out of the office glad for a reprieve. I could see Geoffrey opening his desksafe and pulling out a vial of something as I went out the door.

"I bet he's existing on morphine," I said to Rolf. "That's what's keeping him from total collapse."

"It's so ironic," Rolf stated when we reached Fila's office. "I walk away from a business empire close to 15 years ago and now I'm forced to assume command of an even larger one. And all I want to do is write folk music."

"I know," I sighed. "It's these business types." "All they ever think of is increasing the company assets."

"Their minds are never still not even for a moment, Alvin," Rolf agreed. "Always thinking of how to make the next buck, how to maximize profits, and not caring for a moment about social responsibility."

"That's why I walked away from the business scene," Rolf continued. "My father was just like Enderby. Thinking only of the survival of his business empire."

"But you know there are positive ways of doing business," Rolf remarked. "One of my instructors at Harvard Business School had a different approach to business from the others. A way to conduct business that wasn't necessarily detrimental to others and the environment."

"That's a concept," I remarked. "A way of doing business that's not detrimental to others and the environment. Tell me more."

"Being successful in business doesn't necessarily mean that you can't be socially responsible, Alvin," Rolf continued. "Why some of the most successful businesses practice 'six/six/six' practices."

"Six/six/six practices?"

"On a scale of one to six, most management systems push production at a six, worker morale at one, and social responsibility almost at a minus one," Rolf replied. He went on to tell me that such an approach was the old carrot and stick technique and that one that worked better was a six/six/six grid with worker morale, social responsibility and production all given high priorities. Rolf said that the fellow wasn't given a tenure by the university, but that his system really did work sometimes. He said that he had used it briefly in projects for his father long ago.

I reached for the Orange County files. I was familiar with every one of them.

"There isn't much hope for Enderby's out-of-state projects," I told Rolf. "They're mainly defense projects and I can imagine how a Tibetan Buddhist like you views the military."

Rolf laughed. "All armed forces people think of is winning the war, whatever it is, even if it isn't clear who the enemy is," he commented. He skimmed some of the files but put them down in disgust after half-an-hour.

"Look at this," Rolf said in disgust. "All of the defense projects extract some kind of penalty from the general public, the animal kingdom, or the environment." Rolf told me that the defense project on one of the islands off the coast of Kauai involved placing missile sites among endangered monk seals. He said that two of the defense projects involved sites for toxic waste, despite the protests of native Indian tribes whose land the sites were on, and that another project concerned new sonar systems to monitor enemy submarines using noise echoing, without regard for the effect the noise blasts would have on whale populations and other aquatic animals.

"Not to mention scuba divers," I added.

"At least Fila's projects in Orange Country aren't defense re-lated," I told Rolf. "And Enderby's more worried about hers than the others. Why don't you try and concentrate on Fila's projects while Enderby is alive." I told Rolf that he couldn't tell Enderby to scrap all his defense projects as he was likely to change his mind about naming him the interim CEO. I told him that I suspected that Geoffrey would be open to changes to Fila's projects, and that may be there was some way he could make them more environ-mentally and human friendly.

"Let's see," Rolf glanced at the files. "These three projects are for new shopping centers. That's all Orange Country needs, more shop-ping centers. Promoting increased consumerism isn't at the top of my priorities but what if I suggest changing the emphasis a bit?"

"What do you mean Rolf?" My sense of humor was kicking in. "You're not going to change the lady's projects without consulting her are you? She'll have a hissy fit, you know."

"There are a few, new positive business trends taking place already in California," Rolf commented.

"Like, how about another 'anti-mall', Alvin?" Rolf suggested. "One that's just like the one that is already functioning in Orange County. That type of mall is sort of a protest to normal shopping malls. Giant warehouses," he explained, "without all the expensive trimmings like ambience and interior decor. Just bare walls, high shelving, and products that are enviromentally friendly, like clothes made from hemp. I bet there's room for another 'anti-mall' in Orange County."

. "Oh, that's likely to get Fila's attention," I commented. "That mall was one of her pet projects."

"Forget Fila, Alvin. Perhaps, there is a way I can be a force for good here, like Zot says. Now, these two projects are tourist related," he pulled their files. "A game farm and an undersea aquarium."

Rolf suggested that although there was more loss of agricultural land he could alter the project and suggest that the game farm leave some of the agricultural space to grow vegetables and other food stuffs for its animals. He said the new Disney showplace was already doing that. He said he would suggest the same for the aquarium because it could grow edible sea weeds and use aquaculture techniques to feed it's inhabitants, and that both strategies should save operating costs in the long run.

"Those are two more of the lady's pet projects, Rolf. She won't appreciate not being consulted about them," I warned.

"Let this be our little secret, Alvin," Rolf winked at me.

"Rolf, you're just as diabolical in your own way as Geoffrey," I warned. "The lady will have a kitten at those changes."

"Four of Fila's new projects are related to expansion of the Internet business system, Alvin. What if the designers try and build in a way that allows myriads of little guys to display their wares and prevent large business monopolies from occurring? I don't imagine that can be that difficult. The government hasn't found a way to control the Internet yet, anyway."

"You're incorrigible, Rolf!" I said.

CHAPTER 11.

Honeymoon in Waikiki.

Well, Nordquist went through the marriage ceremony after all, I cursed as I lay in bed admiring the ability of my new wife Daphne to fall asleep under any circumstances.

My hopes rose when a Buddhist Lama appeared to conduct a wedding blessing. I didn't think Nordquist would go through with it. I imagined that Buddhist ceremonies are just as binding as Christian ones. Nordquist looked like he was going to bolt out of the door but I guess the temptation to take over a multi-million dollar business empire was too much for him in the long run, the bastard.

Father is so diabolical. Imagine him augmenting the Justice of the Peace that Alvin had arranged with a High Tibetan Buddhist Lama. Had him flown all the way in from Dharamsala, for God's sake.

Now Nordquist is stuck with my sister and Daphne can't just run off if she gets wind of any of the discreet flirtations I might just happen to indulge in sometime in the future if she starts disagreeing with me too often. I was already angry at Daphne's increasing tendency to correct me. I laughed heartily for the first time since my return to Newport Beach.

"What are you laughing at, sweetheart?" Daphne asked.

"Oh, sorry, darling," I apologized to my new wife.

"I didn't mean to wake you but I couldn't help but laugh at the expression on Nordquist's face when he had to repeat that marriage blessing in Tibetan. What did he and you promise, do you know? Like love, honor, cherish and obey till death do us part?"

"Something like that, I guess, Drew. I know divorce is hardly heard of in Buddhist countries. But why do you hate Rolf Nordquist so much? He's one of the most responsible folk singers of our time."

"That fortune seeker. I'll never forgive the bastard. Imagine, my father prefers Nordquist over his own son."

"Sweetheart, I realise your father hasn't treated you properly from what you've said. And he's made your life a living hell. Why, from what you've told me, nothing you've ever done has ever seemed to please him. But that's not Rolf Nordquist's fault. Why don't you give him a chance?"

Daphne's words triggered me bigtime. I felt myself fly into a savage rage.

"I forbid you to speak Rolf Nordquist's name ever again, Daphne," I shouted. "And don't tell me what my father's done to me, either, thank you. If I wanted psychoanalysis, I would have married a shrink."

But may be I'll have the last laugh on Rolf Nordquist, my rage ceased suddenly as I realized all I had to do was impregnate Daphne before he impregnated Fila. Boys tended to run in the Enderby family.

"I'm sorry, Daphne," I reached for my new wife and pulled her against me. "You know how sensitive I am about my father."

"Imagine if we have a boy before Fila," I chortled. "Nordquist may remain chief executive officer all right but he's going to have to answer to me. I'll be the owner of the controlling shares of Enderby Developments."

"Is that the reason you married me, Drew? To make sure that you have a chance of inheriting Enderby Developments?"

"No, of course not, sweetheart," I lied to Daphne. She didn't need to know I had originally viewed her as another brief but intense fling. My answer seemed to be convincing to the future mother of my son. Daphne relaxed and cooperated fully until we sucessfully ended another try at becoming doting parents.

"Drew, I'm already three weeks past the date this month's period should have started," Daphne totally blew my mind away. Her words threw me into elation. They were the best news I'd heard for the last 10 years.

"That's wonderful Daphne," I congratulated her. I got up, switched on a light and poured two generous glasses of champagne from the bottle that the hotel had provided in it's bridal suite.

"To the heir to Enderby Developments," I put one of the glasses in Daphne's hand.

"Alcohol is dangerous to a fetus, Drew," she warned. "It can cause brain damage if it crosses over to the placenta during crucial stages of development."

"Drink up, the kid doesn't have to be a genius, sweetheart, just as long as it's a boy. That's all we need."

"I want you to see a doctor first thing this morning, Daphne," I commanded. "And have a pregnancy test done. I can't wait to see the look on my sister's face when I tell her you're pregant. Imagine, Nordquist may have to start taking orders from me as soon as eight months from now. Maybe even immediately if father knows you're pregnant before Fila."

Daphne put down her glass without drinking.

"Oh don't bother drinking that, sweetheart." I sensed I was irritating her. I reached for her wine goblet. "Of course I don't want a brain-damaged kid."

"We've got to take every precaution not to lose the kid, Daphne. Look, I'm going to discontinue having sex with you until the kid is born. And I want you to find another jockey to ride your horses at the Derby in a month. I don't want your pregnancy ruined by jarring or injury."

Daphne gasped.

"I can't do that Drew, with Rainbow's End. You know he just won the Santa Anita Derby. That brought big bucks into our racing stables. Rainbow's End is eligible to enter the Kentucky Derby now. You know nobody but me has ever ridden him."

"Use your other jockey, Leonard, Daphne. He's been doing well on Gypsy Strolling."

"Gypsy Strolling is different from Rainbow's End, Drew." I barely listened to Daphne as she told me how she had bottle fed Rainbow's End when his mother couldn't produce milk, and how she had a special bond with the horse.

"He'll run his heart out for me," she added. "There's not time enough to get him used to another jockey. And I need Leonard to ride Gypsy Strolling. We've already entered him into several important races in California."

"You have no choice, Daphne," I told her. "This kid can make me a multi-millionaire. Nothing is more important to me than your having our boy as safely and as fast as possible. Besides, don't be ridiculous. Jockeys are chosen to ride racehorses at the last minute all the time."

"Drew, Rainbow's End will be at a distinct disadvantage if a strange jockey rides him. And the purse at the Kentucky Derby is close to a million dollars this year. Surely that's worth taking a chance on."

"Look Daphne, I'll hear no more about you riding that horse in the Derby. Just have my son and you can ride all the horses you like for the rest of your life, understand?" My tone of voice must have set Daphne straight. She said no more about the horse.

"Come on, it's dawn," I jumped out of the huge water bed in the luxurious honeymoon suite of the most expensive hotel on Waikiki Beach.

I told Daphne that the surf is up and that since my father had coughed up enough money for a honeymoon for us in Waikiki I was going to take advantage of the surfing opportunities for the week that he had allowed us to be here. I ordered Daphne to go to one of the walk-in clinics in Waikiki and find out for sure if we had hit the jackpot.

"You're supposed to get better acquainted with Rolf Nordquist, Drew," she argued. "That's why your father sent all of us on a double honeymoon to Waikiki."

"You missing a few brain cells or something?" I replied. "Don't you understand Daphne? Once you're confirmed pregnant Rolf Nordquist can go straight to hell for all I care."

I threw a T-shirt and pair of shorts over my bathing suit. I dragged Daphne down into the lobby.

"There's Fila and Rolf," she pointed. "Over in the dining room having breakfast. The least we could do is say hello."

I glanced over at Nordquist and gave a short laugh. If I wasn't mistaken he still had a haunted look on his face.

"You're right, Daphne," I relented. I couldn't resist telling my sister and her gigolo about Daphne's pregnancy.

"We'll go over and you have breakfast with them, if you insist," I directed Daphne. "I'll just say hello and then I'm going to go surfing. I don't want you surfing anyway. It's too strenuous and you might have a bad fall."

Daphne gave me an odd look but led me over to my sister's table.

"Aloha," I said jovially. Nordquist looked at me in shock. We sat down and I helped myself from the carafe of coffee on the table.

"Enjoying Waikiki?" Nordquist said pleasantly to Daphne.

"More than I thought possible," I replied.

"Fila, would you do me a favor this morning?" I said casually to my loving sister.

"What could I possibly do for you Drew?" she asked suspiciously.

"Would you accompany Daphne to one of those walk-in clinics they have here. She needs to have a pregnancy test done and I'd appreciate it if you would keep her company. I want to try out some of the surfing at the beach here."

Fila's cup of coffee she was holding went flying into the air. The waiter rushed over and started mopping up the spill all over the table and Fila's expensive, white sports outfit.

"We'd be glad to accompany Daphne to the clinic," Nordquist managed. To my disappointment, his voice lacked even a trace of the despair he must have been feeling.

"Thanks," I jumped up and went out the back of the lobby and down to the area where they rented surfboards.

"I'll never forget the look Fila had on her face," I chortled. "Serves the bitch right. Imagine father favoring her over me all these years."

"Anyone around here give surfing lessons?" I queried one heck of a beautiful older attendant as she collected the deposit for the board rental.

"I geev surfing lesson," she replied. I sized her up. Her English is terrible but who cares? I thought. There's nothing wrong with her body or her looks. She's gorgeous. And Daphne's going to be out of action for at least eight months, I surmised. Surely she can't expect me to be celibate for that amount of time.

Thank God Daphne is occupied with my sister and pseudo brother-in-law, I gave thanks to the Hawaiian dieties, whoever they were. This lady doesn't need to know that I can surf with the best of them.

"Are you available for the entire morning?" I queried. "I'm such a lummox, I have a feeling I'm going to need very close, hands-on, direct instruction if you know what I mean."

"Sure, all day eef you like, handsome?"

"Believe me, I like what I see." I glanced at her body in open appreciation. "She's almost as gorgeous as Daphne," I judged.

"Till lunch," I advised. Daphne should be back with the results from the clinic by then, I thought.

"Four hours should be enough instruction for now," I added. "At least for this morning. Are you free this afternoon sometime?"

"Fo you, I be free anytime," she advised.

I picked up the board, put my free arm around her upper torso and moved towards the water.

"How about the next five days?" I requested. "Every morning and late afternoon."

"You want daily or hourly rate? You can charge on hotel bill."

"Whatever will pay you the most, beautiful Leilani."

"Name is Kealohapau'ole not Leilani," she protested.

Good, this one has spirit, just like Daphne, I thought. That's why I always prefer slightly older women. They have more spirit. Ones that aren't too easy, that is.

"Kealoha, that means love, doesn't it?"

"Kealohapau'ole mean everlasting love."

"Not everlasting," I warned her. "Just for the next five days and whenever I can manage to return to Hawaii." She smiled but looked off in the distance.

Women never believe what you tell them, I laughed to myself. They are programmed to think they can change you. But they don't know the Enderbys. The Enderbys never change. Just look at my Father, I realised.

"Things are looking better every minute," I thought happiy as the two of us moved off close together in the bright turquoise blue water.

CHAPTER 12.

Complications.

"I'm going to kill myself," the hysteria in my heart was causing me to lose complete reason.

"Daphne is pregnant, the test was positive," I wailed to Rolf as I returned from completing Drew's horrendous chore. "Daphne's gone to their suite to tell Drew now. And the baby is likely to be a boy because boys run in the Enderby family line."

I threw myself on the bed in despair. I gave in to my feelings of enormous defeat and sobbed openly in front of Rolf. He sat down on the bed and let me cry into my pillow for quite a while. Finally, I could feel my shoulders stop shaking slightly and I managed to stifle my sobs somewhat. I sat up and Rolf put his arms around me trying to comfort me.

"You must think me a wimp," I started to sob openly again. "These last few months since father developed lung cancer have been like a nightmare."

"I know how important it is for you to gain control of Enderby Developments," Rolf sympathized. "And it's never easy to lose a parent. I can feel your pain. Even if it's self-inflicted, it's still very real."

"Thanks, Rolf, I think. At least you understand."

He gave me another hug.

"You better watch out Rolf," I warned him, surprised at the warmth he was directing at me. "I'm beginning to think you care about what happens to me."

"Don't underestimate yourself, sweetie," he advised. "You are one hell of an attractive lady. If I wasn't so dedicated to reaching enlightenment in this lifetime I'd be very tempted to romance you for real."

"Don't give me any lecture about Buddhist principles," I warned. Rolf laughed.

"That sounds more like you, Ms. Helmsley."

I started to think furiously. I knew I had to come up with a solution immediately or Drew was going to come out in control of Enderby Developments. I could sense that the fact Daphne was already pregnant would give Drew tremendous lobbying power with my father. I was firmly convinced that Drew would destroy the company in less than a year if father allowed him any decision-making responsibility. He was all ego and he just did not have any business sense. Rolf's power as chief executive officer, even if I could somehow get him to stay on, would be seriously under-mined after Father's death if Drew was openly antagonistic.

"You've lost a battle, not a war," Rolf advised, thoughtfully.

"Exactly. Hand me the phonebook will you?"

I reached for the yellow pages and looked up the phone numbers of gynecologists. I found what I was looking for. An advertisement for guaranteed results or your money back. I dialed the number.

"I'm going to cut down the odds a little, Rolf."

"How, Fila?" His voice sounded suspicious.

"Fertility pills. I'm phoning one of the gynecologists that guar-antees pregnancy." Rolf freaked.

"Fila, we could have more than one child if you take fertility pills. I don't want the responsibility of that."

"Don't be ridiculous Rolf," I told him.

"I need an immediate appointment with Dr. Imura," I said into the telephone as a voice answered. "We're only in Hawaii for a week. I need a prescription for fertility pills."

"Mr. & Mrs. Rolf Nordquist," I relayed the information. I noticed Rolf wince at the use of our married names. "Three o'clock, today. Yes, that will be fine."

"You'll send a cab? Very good. Tell Dr. Imura that time is of the essence," I commanded. I gave the receptionist the hotel name, our room number and hung up the phone.

"By the way, thanks for going through the wedding ceremony, Rolf. Believe me, I had no idea that my father was going to add that High Lama from Dharamsala for a wedding blessing."

"Nothing personal, Ms. Helmsley but that blessing freaked me right out. I'm not quite sure what we promised in it. I've got to get it translated somehow. I'm afraid it's a way more binding than the civil ceremony used by Justices of the Peace."

"Don't worry about it, Rolf. I'll leave you, that should get you off the hook. But right now, I have more pressing concerns on my mind."

"You remembered the proverb about the hare and the tortoise?" Rolf sounded odd. He was staring hard at something out the window.

"Precisely. I'm not ready to give up the ship, yet, At least not without a final battle."

"Good for you, Ms. Helmsley," he congratulated me. I don't want Drew to take over Enderby Developments any more than you do. Take a look out the window."

I walked over to the window Rolf found so interesting. He pointed down at the beach directly in front of the hotel. I looked down. Drew was sitting on the sand tightly embracing some attractive, local woman who was somewhat older than him. They were all but making love in public seemingly oblivious to the looks of passerbys."

"Isn't that one of the surf board rental people?" Rolf gasped.

"Oh my God," I cried. "Another older women. So soon after his marriage. I can't believe it?"

"Drew's behaviour is approaching the pathological, Fila. where do you think his obsession with older women comes from?"

"Our mother died when Drew was only 10, Rolf. Suddenly in an automobile accident. Drew was very much a spoiled mother's boy. She protected him from father's anger and his unrelenting

criticisms. Her death threw Drew into the crucible of father's unrelenting efforts to make Drew in his own image. I'm not a psy-
chiatrist but I suspect that had something do do with Drew's attraction to older women."

"He's looking for the unconditional approval your mother gave
him but not his father?"

"Something like that, I guess, Rolf."

"I only hope Daphne's suite doesn't overlook this beach. And
that she hasn't gone looking for the bastard."

"May be someone else needs to know about this," I commented. I reached for my camera and removed the cover off it's
super zoom lens. I snapped several pictures of Drew's activies.

"This camera is one of our wedding presents from father," I
laughed. "I didn't realise it was going to come in so handy."

"You're going to show those pictures to Daphne?" Rolf said,
his voice full of disapproval.

"No, to my Father," I corrected.

"Jesus," Rolf exclaimed. "That might kill him. You know how
much he's deteriorated."

"We have to go down to the lobby, Rolf. Dr. Imura's office is
sending a cab over to pick us up. I've got an appointment for a
preliminary examination for us.

"You don't let any grass grow under your feet do you?"

"Time is the one thing I don't have available, Rolf." He nodded understandingly.

CHAPTER 13.

Return to Newport Beach.

I thanked Lama Tsot for seeing me so quickly as I encountered him at the entrance to his Dharma Center. I felt like I had to talk to someone I could trust about the problem I was having with my husband Drew. It was pulling me in two and I didn't know what to do.

"No problem, Daphne. Lama Tsot glad be able help you. Wat matter?" he replied.

"It's the Kentucky Derby, Lama Tsot," I explained.

"Derby? Wat is Derby?"

"The most prestigious horse race in America. I've done nothing the last 10 years but look for colts that I thought had a possibility of winning the race."

"Winning race?" Lama Tsot looked perplexed.

"You know, Horse racing. Horse owners and their jockeys compete with each other for a large sum of money in races."

"Oh, dat like yak races in Tibet."

"I imagine so." I explained to Lama Tsot that before I had met Drew I was sure Rainbow's End and Gypsy Strolling were going to place in the Kentucky Derby this year, and how I was winning important races with them back in Kentucky. I told him that because both horses were among the best I had ever seen I had invested every cent I had, and even mortgaged my house to purchase and train them.

"And then Drew came along," I explained.

"Your husband Drew?"

"Yes, Lama Tsot." I confessed to the Lama that I'd had many men chasing me in my life, but that all they had wanted was a good time. I told him how I got really hurt twice, falling in love with charming hunks only to have them leave me when I tried to press for some kind of committment.

"Hunks, wat hunks, Daphne?"

"You know, Lama Tsot," I replied. I told him that hunks were men with muscles and strong physique but not necessarily brains. I told the Lama how I had vowed to myself that I wouldn't get close to those types again, but that Drew had been different. I told him that I could tell that Drew was really attracted to me, because, after all he had ignored our age difference and out of the blue proposed. Drew was the only fellow I had met since I was old enough to date that loved me enough to propose marriage, but that his proposal had thrown me for a loop.

"You had decide win Derby or marry Drew?"

"I thought so at first, Lama Tsot." I explained that when I told Drew I couldn't leave racing, Drew promised me that I wouldn't have to because his father would help me relocate my racing stable. I told the Lama that I had realised I could get my horses into the Derby by winning select races in California, and that Geoffrey Enderby had arranged for me to become a member of the Del Mar racing group.

"That's what has been keeping me so busy," I explained. "I'm so proud of my horses."

"Horses win, Daphne?" he asked.

"Yes, Lama Tsot," I replied. "Since you blessed my stable I've had nothing but good luck."

"Wat way?"

I told Lama Tsot how Drew's father was influential in getting me established in other California racing circles as well as Del Mar, and that Gypsy Strolling was doing good by winning several races since I had arrived. I told Lama Tsot that Rainbow's End had been outstanding by winning several key races and that my latest victory on him at the Santa Anita Derby, just before Drew and I left for Hawaii, guaranteed him a chance in the Kentucky Derby.

"Dat wonderful Daphne but wat problem?" Lama Tsot answered.

"Drew says there's no way I can ride in the Derby myself, Lama Tsot." I explained. Tears came to my eyes as I remembered my new husband's totally unexpected order.

"I've never had another jockey riding Rainbow's End. I bottle-fed him when his mother couldn't produce milk and he and I have the most unbelievable bond. He'll do anything for me."

I told Lama Tsot that I was having negative thoughts about Drew. I relayed how I was beginning to think that Drew had married me just to please his father because if Drew really loved me he wouldn't forbid me to ride in the Derby since he knew how much it meant to me.

"Why Drew not want you ride, Daphne?"

"I'm pregnant, Lama Tsot," I confided. I explained how Drew was afraid that I could lose the baby if I rode in the race, and how I could see now that I was over my initial infatuation that Drew wasn't psychologically in good shape. I told Lama Tsot that Drew had too many issues connected to his father that he hadn't been able to deal with. I explained that Drew was stubborn and that he wouldn't listen to me even though I told him he was being over protective. I explained that I had known other female jockeys who had ridden in the early stages of pregnancy and explained that it didn't matter as long as they were in shape to start with.

"And I haven't gained any weight yet," I added. "I can still come in under the maximum 113 pounds allowed for the Derby."

"Baby important you, Daphne?"

"Of course, Lama Tsot. That's one of the reasons I married Drew. My last chance to have a child. But so is riding in the Derby." I choked as I felt myself overcome by emotion at the stress I was feeling.

"Drew says to find another jockey but all the best jockeys are already assigned for the race. I'm not going to trust Rainbow's

End to some second-rate jockey who might even injure him. God knows he's not used to anyone riding him but me."

"We do 'Phowa' Daphne. Transfer consciousness Buddha fields. Ask fo help."

I went over to the meditation pillows in front of Lama Tsot's altar in his office.

"You have initiation fo Green Tara, Daphne? Or Chenrezi initiation?"

"I think so, Lama Tsot. They are called something else, though, in Cambodian Buddhism."

"Buddha's fo compassion," he explained.

"I'm certain I received the initiation to use their mantras and contact them."

"Good. I chant mantra fo Green Tara. Just try relax, Daphne, empty mind," he advised. "Picture Green Tara in mind, say Cambodian mantra fo her. Den place offerings in mind before Buddhas. I try see wat most important fo you."

I relaxed and tried to still my mind as the Master Cambodian Buddhist I had trained under back home had taught. I remembered the words to contact the Goddess of Compassion. Lama Tsot chanted a long mantra in Tibetan interspersed by cymbal clanging and drumming. Before long I sensed the presence of the Goddess. I mentally put offerings of rice, flowers and candles in front of her. Then I imagined myself becoming her as I had been taught. I could feel Lama Tsot directing energy to me and it wasn't long before the pain and fear in my heart about Rainbow's End seemed to dissipate. After some time I realised that Lama Tsot was saying the dedication of the session to all sentient beings that signalled the end of the 'Phowa' and I opened my eyes at his final cymbal strike.

He beamed at me.

"Green Tara give Lama Tsot answer. Lama Tsot ride Rainbow's End in Derby fo you Daphne."

I gasped.

"Not worry Daphne," Lama Tsot saw my look of disappointment. "Lama Tsot good rider. Race many times. Win wild Yak races all time. Lama Tsot best yak racer in all Tibet."

I stared at the Lama in horror.

"I don't want to be a bother, Lama Tsot." I tried to get the well meaning Lama to reconsider. I was sure it wasn't possible to transfer whatever riding training he had in Tibet over to race track riding in America.

"You have believe, Daphne. Green Tara say Lama Tsot ride in Derby, win fo sure. Must have faith."

"What about your students, Lama Tsot? I tried to divert him. I went over my list of second and third-rate available jockeys in my mind. "Don't they need you here?"

"Students come shopping center hours, Daphne. Only open at 9:30 a.m. Rolf's wife, Fila, give Lama Tsot car for use. Students show how drive. Lama Tsot come your stable 5:00 every morning till have go Derby. Train every morning. Students will manage fo week of Derby."

"Do Lamas have a special way with animals?" I asked Lama Tzot. His eagerness seemed to be contagious. I found myself hoping that may be the Lama could ride my racehorse. Somehow, I wanted to believe that Green Tara had actually found a way out of my predicament for me.

"You see, Daphne. We go stables now."

I drove Lama Tsot out to my racing stable. Leonard, my other jockey, had Gypsy Strolling out exercising on the track. Rainbow's End was waiting for me in the exercise paddock. He whinnied at me looking expectantly at the track. My heart sank. It was the first time I had a horse that was so eager to compete and I was forbidden to ride him. Leonard came over and dismounted from Gypsy Strolling.

"Leonard, get me my saddle and bridle, will you?" I directed. "Lama Tsot is going to ride Rainbow's End."

"In those clothes?" Leonard gasped.

"We'd better get you a change of clothes, Lama Tsot," I ordered. I grabbed a clean set of my riding clothes for the Lama.

"Try these for now," I directed. "We can always have some riding clothes made to order." Lama Tsot went over to the changing room.

"Are you really going to let him ride Rainbow's End Daphne?" Leonard queried. "If you ask me you're too over protective of that horse. Why, you won't even let me up on his back."

"Rainbow's End is like my own baby, Leonard. And you need to have faith in a genuine Tibetan Buddhist Lama. They can do the most amazing things." I tried to find a little faith of my own.

Lama Tsot came out in my riding clothes. I looked at his transformation in amazement.

"Well, you are the right size for a jockey," I suppose. "We even probably weigh about the same."

Lama Tsot smiled reassuredly.

"Come with me, Lama Tsot. We'll get you acquainted with Rainbow's End." I led the Lama into the exercise paddock. He was chanting something in Tibetan. I took my riding crop and pointed it at Rainbow's End. He started trotting obediently around the paddock like I had conditioned him to do in his early training stages. Then I signalled him to return to me. He obediently ran up and I gave him a sugar cube from my hand. I hugged him on his head and he whinnied.

"Now you do the same, Lama Tsot." I handed the riding crop to the Lama and stepped out of the paddock. Rainbow's End whinnied anxiously. Lama Tsot said something to the horse in Tibetan. The horse seemed to calm down. Lama Tsot gave the signal with the riding crop for Rainbow's End to trot around the paddock. The horse glanced at me as if asking if this was for real. I motioned for him to go. Lama Tsot gave the riding crop signal again and Rainbow's end complied. He obediently trotted around the exercise paddock.

After a few minutes Lama Tsot signalled the large, bay, three-year old to return to him and Rainbow's End went over obediently. Lama Tsot gave him a sugar cube and hugged him just as I had done. I moved in and placed my bridle, blanket and saddle on Rainbow's End.

Lama Tsot stepped confidently into the stirrups and lifted himself into the saddle. My big, bay, horse stared at me as if questioning me again. I gave him a big hug and told him to do his best just like I always did. Lama Tsot turned the bridle and pressed the riding crop onto Rainbow's End. To my shock, Rainbow's End trotted around the paddock just like he would have done for me.

After several minutes, I opened the paddock's gate. "See if he'll go over to the starting gate," I shouted to Lama Tsot. He directed the horse towards the starting gate.

"Just ride him slowly through the race track," I directed Lama Tsot. The Lama nudged him forward and the two of them went slowly around the course without a problem.

"Leonard, take Gypsy Strolling into the starting gate," I directed my other jockey. My heart was beating furiously. Rainbow's End was tolerating a rider other than myself, something he'd refused to do before.

As Lama Tsot returned from around the course again I directed him into the gate next to Leonard.

"Now we'll see if there's any possibility of this working," I mentally decided.

When the horses were abreast I deployed the starting gate. Both horses surged forward down the track. I couldn't believe my eyes.

Lama Tsot immediately gained the lead. Rainbow's End was nearly a length ahead of Gypsy Strolling. I realised the Lama had not been wrong about his riding ability. He was showing perfect form.

"Do your best, Leonard," I yelled. Leonard struck his riding crop on Gypsy Strolling's backside. He moved a little closer to Rainbow's end. Both horses were nose to nose as they rounded the first turn. They stayed neck to neck to the half-way point as both furiously fought with each other for the lead. Then Leonard on Gypsy Strolling gained about a two-length lead. As they approached the final turn Leonard had stretched his lead to three lengths. Lama Tsot furiously pressed his crop onto Rainbow's end and my best horse surged forward. He kept on creeping up on Gypsy Strolling. At the finish line Rainbow's End won by a nose.

"Why, I think that Lama even rides better than you do, Daphne," Leonard shouted in shock.

"I hope you're right, Leonard," I answered. "Lama Tsot is going to ride Rainbow's End in the Kentucky Derby. And you can continue entering Gypsy Strolling in California races."

"Why aren't you riding Rainbow's End?" Leonard demanded in shock.

"I'm pregnant, Leonard. My husband doesn't want me to risk losing the baby."

"Geez!" Leonard muttered. He led the horses around to the exercise area to cool them off.

"Lama Tzot, you did great. But what if Rainbow's End does by some miracle place or win at the Derby. The next race of the Triple Crown, the Preakness is two weeks later. Are you going to be able to take enough time off for that?"

"Students manage, Daphne. New Lama from Dharamsala come soon. Take students on retreat, mountains. Dey learn subdue ego. Not rely on Lama Tsot always. Good fo dem."

"Lama Tsot. You can't ride Rainbow's End all out in the Derby like you just did here. He's what's called a 'speed horse.' He can sprint incredibly fast for short distances but you've got to keep him from running all out for the full Derby race course."

"Wat you mean, Daphne."

I explained how the Derby was a mile-and-a-quarter and how that was more than Rainbow's End had ever run. I explained how he would have to ride with 'a clock in his head,' which meant that Lama Tsot had to know exactly where he was located and and how far there was to go yet.

"Lama Tsot understand." he said. "Same in some yak races. Stay wit front runners but wait for opening near end race and then give everyting."

"That's right, Lama Tsot," I told him. "That's called 'choosing the optimal moment and finding a hole.' It's the strategy I was going to use for the Derby."

"Lama Tsot do dat Daphne. Win fo sure."

May be there is time to teach Lama Tsot most of what I know about racing in time for the Derby, I thought. My spirits lifted for the first time since the wedding.

May be I don't have to defy Drew and ride in the race like I was going to do, I realised. Maybe there is hope for this marriage. I thought of my unborn child.

I hope the baby is a girl, I thought. I don't want my baby to grow up like Drew. Never able to meet his father's impossible career expectations if he's a boy.

CHAPTER 14.

The Race.

I found myself taking a big sigh as I sat down in the stands on the day of the Kentucky Derby. Geoffrey Enderby had flown all of us out to Churchill Downs to watch Rainbow's End run in the race. Drew and Daphne were somewhere taking care of last minute preparations. I glanced at the huge crowd as far as the eye could see. Over 140,000 excited souls, the announcer on television claimed. I was plugged into a small handset as even in the clubhouse, it was difficult to get a view of everything. I could barely see the 60,000 fans herded like sheep into the infield. The most they could hope to see from there was glimpses of the race. A real carnival atmosphere prevailed. I could feel the surge of emotion that was present around the race track. Anxiety filled the faces of trainers, jockeys and owners. Even the horses were likely to be affected by the bustle and noise as they had to pass through the smells of barbecues and cheers of celebrants as their keepers took the horses from the barns on their way to the parade around the first turn.

Alcohol was flowing freely all over as many were drinking the traditional mint juleps in frosted souvenir glasses. The race was sold out. I could see celebrities, wearing their finest, filling the most expensive seats around us. Huge lineups were formed around the betting wickets. I had already placed large bets on Rainbow's End for Fila and her father.

"Imagine Zot riding in the race for Daphne, darling?" Alvin said to Fila.

"I find that really hard to believe, Alvin. Do you actually think that Rainbow's End has any chance at all to win?"

"Well, Daphne swears it's possible, darling," he answered. "And Rainbow's End is one of the favorites for betting." Alvin told us that once racing fans got over the initial shock of seeing Zot in his orange and red robes, they decided that the presence of a Buddhist Lama as a jockey was a lucky sign.

"I told you how important a good makeover is," he said.

"Rainbow's End went from being a longshot at 50 to one to the favorites for the race," I added.

"There's Lama Tsot," Alvin exclaimed. I stared at Zot and all the jockeys as the little television screen in my hand displayed the traditional photo. Zot was beaming ear to ear.

"Now that's style," Alvin commented.

"Yeah, Zot looks all right in those red and orange racing clothes," I laughed. "Daphne had them especially made for him."

Why he looks stunning," Alvin corrected. "Psychedelic is the latest trend in America and those red and orange shirt and pants are psychedelic."

Fila chuckled.

"I never foresaw that Daphne would be this successful with her horses," she added.

"The report I had done on Daphne when when she turned up in Newport Beach said that she is one of the best trainers in Kentucky as well as one of it's most successful jockeys," Geoffrey Enderby joined the conversation. "Imagine her winning the Santa Anita Derby."

I looked at Enderby with sadness. His condition was deteriorating and even the expert make up job he did on himself couldn't completely cover the ravages of the disease on his face. He been gradually shifting the management decisions for Enderby Developments onto me.

"I'm so glad I've been able to make the trip out here," he beamed. "I'm so grateful for Daphne marrying Drew."

"And so you should be," Alvin commented.

"Didn't you show your father those photographs you took of Drew and the surf-board rental person, sweetie?" I asked Fila when Enderby went off for some mint juleps.

"I thought you had. Drew's not raised a voice against me at the director's meeting since we came back but Enderby seems oblivious to the cracks in Drew's marriage."

"I didn't show those photos to my father, Rolf. I didn't have the heart. I was afraid it might kill him, like you said. I blackmailed Drew with them, instead."

"My God, darling," Alvin exclaimed. "You're developing compassion," Fila turned bright red. "It must be Lama Tsot's influence. What will happen next?"

"Have you got the photos in a safe place, Ms. Helmsley?" I joked. "Drew might be willing to kill for them."

Fila explained that she had to give them and the negatives to Drew to stop his opposition to my business decisions but not to worry. She told Alvin and I how Drew didn't know that she had already had duplicates made of the pictures, and that they were in a safety deposit box is her bank. Fila told us that she could always threaten to show them to Daphne anytime Drew got pushy again. She said that she imagined that Drew was waiting for her father's death now before he made his move.

"How are the fertility pills working, sweetie?" I kept my voice casual. I knew Fila was pretty hysterical about the matter.

"Doctor Jarvis say's I'm pregnant, Rolf."

"That's wonderful, darling," Alvin commented.

I put my arms around Fila. "Are you going to let your father know?"

"I'll tell him after the race, Rolf. I wanted to let you know first."

"Thanks, sweetie." My heart chakra lit up with the news. A strange combination of anxiety and warmth struck me.

I'm going to have a kid, I thought, or kids. Except, I'm just supposed to walk out of their lives. May be I won't even get to see the babies. I was strangely upset at that thought. The future was making me extremely anxious.

"You'd better get Father, Rolf. The crowd is singing 'My Old Kentucky Home' and the horses are moving up to the starting gate."

I located Enderby at the bar and helped him carry back the mint juleps in their frosted glasses.

"Thanks, Rolf," he coughed, trying to hide the spatter of blood on his hankerchief. "I wouldn't miss this race for anything. Daphne's got her heart set on winning it. Do you really think she has a chance with Lama Tsot riding Rainbow's End?"

"You never know," I replied. "Daphne swears he can win it."

"Thank God for you and Daphne. I don't know what I would have done without you two."

I felt a little guilt at my continued deception of the old boy but I knew it was useless to say anything. Enderby still wouldn't consider placing Fila in charge of Enderby Developments.

"This is it," Alvin shouted to Enderby. "I can't believe Lama Tsot is riding Rainbow's End."

There was a blaze of color as the gun sounded and the horses surged forward through the starting gates.

"What a powerful sight," I thought. "All that horse power roaring down the track at 40 miles per hour."

Rainbow's end had drawn post ten and for the first few furlongs he was near the back of the pack of 18 horses. As they rounded the first turn, however, Zot struck his riding crop firmly on Rainbow's End and the horse surged forward. He made his way up through the throng in front of him to seventh place.

"What a blazing pace," the announcer shouted at the halfway point. Zot had moved up slightly but was still behind the front runners. Suddenly the favorite, Crystal Spring, made his move and lunged into the lead. The horses seemed to quickly rearrange their order as they fought furiously for position. Zot found a hole and moved up to fourth place. He was holding it by a nose. My heart pounded as I realised that both Rainbow's End and Zot were managing the frantic pace of the race.

"Go Lama Tsot," Alvin shouted. I realised I had tears in my eyes as Zot suddenly found space on the outside and moved Rainbow's End past the horse running third.

"The horses are flying this last sixteenth of a mile," the announcer shouted.

"Rainbow's End is going to place," Alvin cried.

"My God, he's taken the lead," Enderby shouted as the horse continued to gain speed. He was suddenly one length ahead of the favorite, Crystal Spring.

Both horses were furiously accelerating toward's the finish line. Zot was croutched above the horse striking him lightly with his riding crop.

"Joker's Wild is coming through the pack," the announcer yelled. I glared at the screen. It was suddenly a three-way race. Joker's Wild crept past Crystal Spring. A final surge brought several of the middle horses close to the front runners.

I sighed as both Crystal Spring and Joker's Wild were moving closer to Rainbow's End. Suddenly all three flashed across the wire in a blur. Zot had his arm raised in triumph as he stood to slow Rainbow's End but I couldn't tell if Rainbow's End was actually first.

"It's a photo finish," the announcer cried.

The camera shifted to Daphne running towards the horses. Tears were streaming down her face."

The camera closed in on Zot. He was hugging Daphne's horse and saying something loudly in Tibetan.

A fellow in a bright red English riding jacket suddenly came up to Zot and Rainbow's End. He led the big bay horse towards the winner's circle.

"Rainbow's End has it by a nose," the announcer shouted. Joker's Wild is second and Crystal Spring third." The crowd went wild.

We watched in amazement as the huge blanket of red roses was placed on Rainbow's End.

"Zot's done it," Alvin. "He's won the Kentucky Derby for Daphne."

I reached for my hankerchief. Tears were running down my face.

Everyone was watching the presentation of the cup. Daphne and Drew were both standing next to the race officals. "An incredible win," the official handed the elegant cup with the horse and jockey on top of it to Daphne.

"Welcome back to Kentucky, Daphne!" he said. Drew gave her a congratulatory kiss as the cameras switched to the betting odds.

"Rainbow's End paid $32.23 to one," I laughed to Enderby. "Not bad for a horse that no one realized could possibly win."

"Daphne is well on her way to being a millionaire," Alvin announced incredulously.

"Daphne's made a name for herself in the highest racing circles," Enderby commented. "If she keeps winning races like she is doing she'll be able to command the highest sums for her horses."

"Father, there's something you should know," Fila interrupted.

God, she's not going to show him those photographs of Drew, is she? My heart stopped.

"Rolf and I want you to know that I'm pregnant, Father."

"Congratulations you two!" Enderby beamed. He took all of us into the clubhouse and ordered several bottles of champagne.

"Doctors be damned," he muttered, pouring out generous glasses of champagne for everyone in sight."

"Rolf, surely you can celebrate a happening of this importance?"

"Of course, Geoffrey. Buddhists are allowed the odd drink on special occasions."

"To the unborn children," Enderby held up his wine glass. "May they lead Enderby Developments into the future." We clicked our glasses in triumph.

CHAPTER 15.

The Belmont Stakes.

"What do you mean, you're thinking of withdrawing Rainbow's End from the Belmont Stakes?" Drew shouted at me in disbelief.

"Can't we discuss this in a civilized manner, Drew?" I felt myself drawn in to returning my husband's anger. It had become so tiresome.

"We're about to go to the airport to fly to New York for the race and you change your mind at the last minute. Do you realize what the fee is to fly that animal to New York. And we've already paid the flight expenses. They're not refundable, I assure you."

"Stop shouting, Drew." My pain at the way Drew had been treating me since our marriage surged to the surface. I was so fed up with Drew's frequent excuses for last minute dinner cancellations, his constant criticisms of me when he did turn up, and the way he thought only of his own needs.

"If you were around more you would have realised that it was necessary to do a last minute evaluation of the injury on Rainbow's End leg. The injury that had kept him out of the Preakness." I told Drew that not even the vet was sure if Rainbow's End was ready for the Belmont. I reminded Drew that, if he had been listening to me last week, he would have heard that Lama Tsot wasn't available for the race, and that I had told him that Lama Tsot had been asked to lead a retreat in the woods at Lake Tahoe. I told Drew that people had signed up for the retreat from all over the world.

"What's Lama Tsot got to do with it?" Drew asked. "I thought Leonard was going to race Rainbow's End in the Belmont."

I told Drew that he never listened to me, even during the odd evening when he didn't have to stay late in the office. I relayed to Drew that I had been re-evaluating Leonard's style, and that I was worried that the injury Rainbow's End suffered had not been healing fast enough for him to be run full out in the race.

"Leonard is 'gung ho' to win horseraces," I added. "I'm afraid he won't be able to gauge how far to push Rainbow's End with that injury. I don't want to risk further damage to the horse."

I braced myself as I could see the fury in Drew's eyes. As usual, he's not validating my concerns, I realised.

"For God's sake, Daphne, there's a million dollar purse up for grabs, not to mention the increase in the stud fees if Rainbow's End wins the Belmont as well as the Derby." I couldn't believe my ears as Drew told me that the horse was insured and if he was injured further it wouldn't matter. I winced as he said that even if we had to shoot Rainbow's End, the insurance would cover any purses or future stud fees he would have produced.

"We'll never make it big in racing if you continue to coddle your racehorses," Drew concluded.

"You're still not hearing me, Drew," I shouted. "Leonard's style and Rainbow's End's nature are not compatible, particularly with this injury." I couldn't believe Drew's callous disregard for Rainbow's End. "I insist we withdraw the horse from the race."

"We've got too much invested Daphne. Grab some other jockey," he ordered.

"I suppose I could ride the horse myself, Drew," I replied, "but I don't have the confidence we can race him without risking serious injury."

Drew's face went red with anger.

"How can you think of riding the horse yourself, Daphne? Why, I have the inheritance of Enderby Development's controlling stock riding on the birth of a healthy baby boy. Have you no brain?"

He told me that Leonard was perfectly capable of judging how hard to drive Rainbow's End. He insisted that I use Leonard or another jockey and enter the horse in the Belmont.

I couldn't believe the fury that Drew had in his voice. He looked like he was going to hit me. I lost my cool completely.

"Do you realise what that horse means to me, Drew?" I shouted back. "I'm telling you, the only way I'll enter Rainbow's End in the Belmont is if I ride him myself. Besides, there's no danger to the fetus," I added. I told Drew how I had checked with Dr. Baker and that he had told me that as long as I didn't take any unnecessary risks the ride would go all right. I told Drew that I knew I could trust myself to gauge how far to push Rainbow's End.

"To hell with Dr. Baker!" he shouted. "I'm warning you, Daphne. Use Leonard or get another jockey and enter that horse in the race. If you should be so foolish to withdraw it or ride the horse yourself, you can forget about our marriage. You can just walk out that door and never mind coming back."

I gasped in horror. Now my husband was threatening me to get his own way. I forced myself to calm down a little.

"And another thing, Daphne," Drew shouted. "I want that pagan shrine of yours in our bedroom removed from father's beachhouse." Drew explained how it had always bothered him. I couldn't believe it as Drew forbid me to have anything more to do with Buddhism or Lama Tsot. He declared that he didn't want any child of his indoctrinated into some foreign cult. I exploded.

"Don't you dare tell me I don't have a right to my own religious beliefs, Drew," his words had removed the last vestiges of my self-control. "I'll tell you something," Anger drove me to issue an ultimatum of my own. "You're the one that has a choice to make. Either I ride Rainbow's End or we withdraw him from the race. And forget about attacking my religion. That's not even up for discussion. Make up your mind."

I reminded Drew that Leonard was about to take the horse to the airport for his flight to New York and that Michael was about to drive up with the limo to take us to the airport.

"What have you decided?" I demanded.

I couldn't believe Drew's look of hatred. He raised his hand to strike me. I gasped but managed to keep staring at him without the fear in my heart showing in my eyes. He took a step towards me but then dropped his hand, picked up one of the dining room chairs and slammed it into the wall as hard as he could.

"I can't believe you did that, Drew," I gasped. He stalked out of the room, charged through the dining room and slammed the outside door with all his strength. I jumped as an ear-piercing crash and the sound of glass smashing let me know that the crystal chandelier above the dining room table had come crashing down.

I staggered into the living room and sat down on the chesterfield allowing tears to stream down my face. My anger had given way to self-pity.

Thank God we're alone, I thought. How am I going to explain the chandelier to Fila and Geoffrey Enderby? I don't think they have any idea about the cracks in Drew's and my marriage.

Why do my relationships always have to turn out like this, I sobbed. I have a marked talent for picking loser men. And I thought Drew was different. He's just like all the rest. Thinking only of himself and his own needs.

I'm so tired of Drew's condescending manner, I realised through my pain, and his anger. He uses his anger like a weapon to get his own way. That behaviour is so destructive. And now he's left, forcing me to make the decision about Rainbow's End myself. I might as well be alone. It can't be any worse than this.

The sound of Drew's tires squealing furiously as he roared out of the driveway caused another stab of pain in my heart.

He didn't even bother to investigate the crash, I acknowledged. And threatening to end our marriage if I don't follow his orders. I sobbed for several minutes and then went to the little shrine that Drew had wanted destroyed. I sat down in front of it and chanted the contact mantra for Green Tara. The energy of the goddess reached me immediately and I felt my soaring emotions calm somewhat.

What am I going to do? I asked. I felt myself drawn deeper into a meditative state. Then suddenly I knew without a doubt that I couldn't let Drew's selfishness or his anger control our marriage. I ended the meditation and came back fully to consciousness.

I reached for the telephone on the lamp table in the dining room. I glanced around me in disbelief. Shattered glass was all around. Pieces of it were even impaled in the walls.

What if I had rushed after Drew? I thought. I might have been standing in this room when the chandelier came down.

"Lama Tsot," I recogised the voice of my friend and teacher when I called his center. "Would you mind putting in a word to Green Tara for me and Rainbow's End over the next few days?"

"Wat problem now, Daphne?"

"I'm worried about the injury to Rainbow's End, Lama Tsot. I don't think it's healing fast enough for the race and I'm not sure that Leonard would be able to gauge how far to push the horse without injuring him further." I told the Lama how Drew was furious that I was thinking of either riding Rainbow's End in the Belmont Stakes myself or withdrawing the horse, and how we had gotten into an argument ending with Drew even ordering me to give up Buddhism.

"Drew's gone off in a rage," I explained. "I don't imagine he'll be there for me at the race at all. Drew even told me not to bother coming back to Newport Beach if I withdraw the horse, if I ride the horse myself, or if I don't give up Buddhism."

"You want Lama Tsot cancel retreat, and ride Rainbow's End fo you Daphne? Retreat can be rescheduled, I tink."

"No Lama Tsot. Thank you, but I never should have agreed to Drew's command to step down for the Derby. My doctor says that this early into the pregnancy there's little danger to the fetus. And you've got people coming from all over for the retreat."

"You sure, Daphne?"

"Yes, Lama Tsot. Thank you, but I can see there's something even more important than the Belmont at stake here, the future of my marriage." I told Lama Tsot that if I were to let Drew use his anger as a weapon to control me there would be no hope for future growth for either of us and that my marriage would become a trap instead of the loving partnership I expected it to be.

"I speak goddess Tara, Daphne." The phone went dead for a couple of minutes. I could feel the goddess's energy reach me again and my surging emotions calmed somewhat.

"You sitting down, Daphne?" Lama Tsot's voice returned.

"Yes, Lama Tsot," I assured him.

"Big problem, Daphne. You right. Goddess Tara say problem wit Drew about mo dan just his anger. She say you have face possibility you tink you in love wit Drew when first meet but you mistake physical attraction for love. Same wit Drew."

Tears welled in my eyes. I felt like my heart was breaking. And I felt my face growing beet red.

"I'm beginning to admit that to myself, Lama Tsot," I confessed. "But Drew seemed to be in love with me. He said he was anyway."

"Goddess Tara say now matter of wat called integrity in marriage. You have be true to self, Daphne. Better be alone dan agree to tings you no tink right. No one have right dictate wat you believe. Must decide dat fo self. Tink your husband need find way control his anger and listen to udders or all his life people around him suffer. He much worse dan his fadder."

"I've got to go to the airport, Lama Tsot, if I'm going to make that flight. I promise I'll think about what you've said. Please contact Green Tara for me over the next few days?"

"Of course, Daphne. Good luck in Belmont if you decide enter. Lama Tsot, all retreat people be cheering fo you."

"Thanks, Lama Tsot."

I walked to the hallway of Geoffrey Enderby's beach house and separated my luggage from Drews. I debated taking his ticket from the travel package.

May be he'll relent and meet me at the airport, I felt myself hoping. No, I reasoned. When Drew gets angry like that he stays angry for hours, sometimes days. He goes into some kind of obsession about his perceived injustices.

I left Drew's ticket on the dining room table by the crashed chandelier. The heavy oak table had withstood the crash although

I imagined it was badly dented. I gathered up my Buddhist implements and small statue of the Goddess Tara and put them in one
of my suitcases. I gathered up some of my clothes I had brought
from Kentucky and packed them. I unpacked the expensive jew-
elry Drew had given me throughout our marriage. I put it in the
wall safe in the living room. "Take these suitcases out to the driveway, will you, Michael, and have the others returned to the bedroom?" I ignored the curious look on Geoffrey Enderby's butler's
face as he arrived with the limo to take us to the airport. Drew's
father had insisted we go in style.

What's this going to do to Geoffrey? I wondered. A stab of
pain went through my heart.

His condition has deteriorated so much lately. He's barely been
able to make it to the office. What if I don't come back? Geoffrey
thinks that our marriage has transformed his son into a responsible businessman. He's so grateful. If I don't come back from Kentucky the shock might kill him. He's lost so much weight lately.

Thank heavens, none of the servants or Fila were present to
hear that argument, I thought.

"By the way, there's been a minor earthquake or something,
Michael. The chandelier came crashing down onto the dining room
table. Perhaps, you can get someone in to repair the damage?"

"Certainly, Madam," Michael gasped. "After I drive you and
young Mr. Enderby to the airport?"

"My husband won't be accompanying me to the Belmont
Stakes, Michael. He's had something come up at the office," I lied.

"I'll advise Mr. Enderby, Madam."

I went out of the luxurious beach house that Drew insisted we
stay in and sat down heavily in the back seat of Geoffrey Enderby's
limo that Drew expected to inherit.

I hate all this opulence, I acknowledged to myself as Michael
loaded the suitcases and we drove to the airport.

I've been fooling myself about this marriage. It's become a
sham, I acknowledged. I thought of Drew's words. "Don't bother
coming back," he had said. May be I won't have to come back and

continue to be Mrs. Drew Enderby, I caught myself wishing. I thought of my husband's ultimatum.

God knows Drew hardly spends any time with me anyway. Between my horse races and his military projects, we hardly see each other.

And he never comes home for dinner, I realised I was fed up with rushing home from the stables to make the 7:00 p.m. time for the family gathering that Geoffrey Enderby insisted on only to hear that Drew still had to take care of something with his administrative assistant at the office.

This is too depressing, I willed myself to stop evaluating my marriage. I went into meditation and sounded the mantra to summon the goddess Tara again. My spirits lifted as I felt the energy of the goddess all around me.

What a way to enter the Belmont, I thought as I checked into the airport terminal. I went straight to the airport gate and sat in the front row for the boarding call. Within 20 minutes I knew my assessment of my husband had been correct. The boarding call for the first class passengers had arrived and Drew was nowhere in sight. I moved onto the plane in deep grief.

I'm not going to let Drew's anger ruin my life, I vowed as I took my seat. It's better to be alone, like Lama Tsot says, than live with someone I'm not really in love with, or to compromise everything I believe in, I decided. I wonder what we promised to that High Lama in the Buddhist blessing of our marriage? I'll have to ask Lama Tsot the next time I'm talking to him. I'm not sure I'm prepared to put up with some spoiled, immature, jerk with bad judgement that wants his own way at all costs.

I tried to put all thoughts of Drew out of my mind. I knew I needed all my wits to decide on what to do about Rainbow's End.

Thank God, Fila's secretary Alvin advised me to make sure both my horses were listed as my assets in the pre-nuptial agreement, I thought suddenly.

Imagine what control Drew would have if the horses were part of the assets of the stable. He knows how much I love those horses.

I thought of Gypsy Strolling. He was still at the stable.

What if Drew is serious about my not coming back? I thought suddenly. I might have to keep Rainbow's End in New York or may be return to Kentucky with him. May be I should have Gypsy Strolling shipped out to Kentucky, my thoughts whirled. Before he gets taken hostage by Drew.

I must be developing paranoia, I tried to calm my pounding heart. Surely, things can't be that bad.

You poor little kid, I said to my unborn child. Imagine having to deal with a father like Drew.

I've got to contact a lawyer, I realised. How could I have been so mistaken about Drew and myself. I thought we loved each other but I must have been delusional or something. You would think I would be able to evaluate men by this time in life.

I've got to stop these thoughts, I told myself. Somehow I've got to figure out what to do about Rainbow's End.

By the time I reached New York I was a basket case. I took a cab to the luxurious hotel that Drew had booked and went straight to my room. The opulence of the luxury hotel did nothing to improve my mood. It reminded me of Geoffrey Enderby's house in Newport Beach. Impulsively, I phoned Enderby Developments head office and asked for Rolf Nordquist.

"Who shall I say is calling?" his secretary requested.

"It's his doctor's office," I lied. I didn't want Drew getting wind of what I was doing. The secretary put me right through to Rolf.

"Aloha, Dr. Gibbons," he said warmly.

"Rolf, it's not your doctor, its Daphne, Drew's wife."

"Daphne," he said sounding startled. "I thought you and Drew were flying to New York for the Belmont.

"Rolf, are you alone? Can anyone hear you?" I demanded.

"I'm in Fila's office, alone, Daphne, Alvin's not even here," he replied. "What's wrong? I can hear the anxiety in your voice."

"I am in New York but I've had a dreadful argument with Drew. I need your advice."

"Of course. Anything I can do, I'll be glad to do it for you."
I relaxed slightly as I knew Rolf wasn't just being polite.

"Drew flew into a rage this morning when I tried to discuss
my withdrawing Rainbow's End from the Belmont." I told Rolf
how the cut on the horse's leg was kind of iffy and that I didn't
want the horse running all out if he was entered. I told Rolf that
my jockey Leonard's style was not compatible with that kind of
racing and that the only other alternative was to ride the horse
myself. I told Rolf how Drew had told me to forget our marriage if
I either rode the horse myself or withdrew him from the race, and
how he had also ordered me to leave Buddhism.

"He said my small shrine in our bedroom was freaking him
out and he wasn't going to have a child of his indoctrinated in
some weird, foreign cult," I added.

"Drew said all that, Daphne, and he wouldn't hear of withdrawing the horse?" Rolf sighed.

"Not only that, he flew off in a rage and slammed the front
door so hard the chandelier came crashing down onto the dining
room table. Please explain that to Fila for me, will you?"

"Didn't Drew apologise?"

"No, he wasn't listening to anything but his own voice," I
complained. "I'm completely shaken up about my marriage. I don't
think Drew really loves me and I think I might have been inter-
preting physical attraction as love when I first met Drew." I told
Rolf that the only emotions that Drew seemed to be arousing in
me now were anger and fear, and that he seemed to be more into
control than anything else. I told Rolf that all Drew seemed to
care about was money, and having a son to inherit Enderby Developments' controlling stock. I even confessed that I suspected that
the only reason Drew married me was to please his father. I asked
Rolf what he thought I should do?

"Daphne, you've got to protect yourself," Rolf advised. "You
need to see a lawyer right away."

"I know," I sobbed. "I think I'm developing paranoia or something, but I'm even worried about my other racehorse, Gypsy Stroll-

ing. Do you think I should make arrangements about shipping him to New York, too, or may be Kentucky? I have friends there that could board him and keep him safe."

"If it relieves your mind, Daphne, make arrangements to have the horse shipped to your friends in Kentucky, and see a lawyer. You need to protect your assets in your racing stable and you need to consult someone about custody rights to your unborn child if Drew is serious about your not coming back."

"Right now, in the middle of last minute preparations for the race?"

"I don't want to panic you further, Daphne, believe me, but I don't think Drew is very stable. If he gets any idea that you might be thinking of a divorce yourself, he's capable of doing anything."

"You're not very reassuring, Rolf."

"I know, Dear." Rolf told me that he was going to get tickets for a flight to New York for Fila and himself. He said that he didn't think that I needed to be all alone in the crisis right now. Rolf asked permission to consult Geoffrey Enderby and Enderby Development's head lawyer about the situation as he thought the company's interests were at stake now as well as my personal happiness.

"In confidence, of course," he asked.

"You would do that for me, Rolf," I gasped.

"Fila and I will be out there tomorrow at the latest, Daphne. Just go on with your racing preparations. What hotel are you staying at?"

"The Ritz. Suite 321."

"If Drew calls, just tell him you still haven't decided what to do or who's going to ride Rainbow's End. Tell him you're trying to make last minute arrangements. We want to give him a chance to get his anger under control."

"Thanks, Rolf," I told him.

CHAPTER 16.

Crisis In New York State.

"Fila," I shouted as I rushed into the Newport Beach House.

"Up here, Rolf," she answered. "In the baby's room." I raced up the stairs.

What a lovely sight, I stopped in my tracks as I entered the room. Fila had all the baby's toys, furniture and decorations set up. Even the colorful mural that a baby could stare at from inside the crib was in place. I looked at my wife and smiled. She was sitting in a meditative state on the floor reading Dr. Spock. I gasped as Fila looked lovelier than I'd ever seen her.

"You look beautiful, Ms. Helmsley," I teased her as I went over to her side. She put her face towards me expectantly and I found myself kissing her tenderly on the lips.

"Even at four months pregnant?" she asked.

"The baby or babies is bringing out the best in you, sweetie," I advised her. "Even your inner self seems changed. You seem so much more at peace with yourself and the world."

"Rolf," Fila answered. "The doctor isn't saying anything about multiple births."

"Yet!"

"What's up?" she asked. "You don't usually rush home in the middle of the day."

"There's a crisis with Drew and Daphne, sweetie. I've conferred with your father about it." I brought Fila up to date on the crisis.

"Drew got quite nasty about the whole thing," I added. "He insisted the horse be entered in the race, and told Daphne not to come back if either she withdraws Rainbow's End, rides him herself or insists on remaining a Buddhist."

"Rolf, Daphne shouldn't be riding a racehorse. She must be close to five months pregnant," Fila said.

"I know sweetie, but I wasn't going to tell her that. She's in tears in a hotel room in New York. I told her we would take the next plane out there to be with her. I hope you agree."

"Of course. It must be her hormones from the pregnancy, Daphne is usually so calm and controlled."

"Drew did a good imitation of Dr. Jekyll and Mr. Hyde. According to Daphne, he almost struck her. I understand the chandelier in your father's dining room even came crashing down when he slammed the front door."

"That's what happened to it. Michael said a small earthquake had struck."

I helped Fila to her feet.

"I've got tickets for the three o'clock flight, sweetie. We'll just make it if we throw some things into a suitcase and leave now."

"How's father taking this? He has so much hope for Drew because of this marriage."

"Not well, sweetie." I told Fila how her father had told me to go with her and see if we could smooth things out for Drew. I told her that her father was conferring with the Enderby Developments' lawyers about what to do about the baby if Daphne didn't come back.

"Did you contact Lama Tsot, Rolf?" I couldn't believe my wife's question.

"He knows all about it, Sweetie. Zot says that this crisis is about more than the horse race. He says it's about integrity in relationships or marriage. About being true to one's beliefs. And how Drew uses anger to control those around him."

"Where is Drew in all this?"

"I don't know, sweetie. Your father couldn't track him down. He booked out of the office for a couple of weeks for the race. Nobody's seen or heard from him at the office since this morning when Daphne says he left the driveway in a rage. His administrative assistant wasn't available, either."

"May be he's come to his senses and is flying to New York?"

"We'll see when we get there." My wife was surprising me again. Fila seemed genuinely concerned about Drew as well as Daphne.

"Something's happened to Ms. Helmsley," I realised. I helped Fila pack and we went out to her high-powered sedan. I settled Fila in the front seat noticing that I had to adjust her seatbelt again to her fast growing waistline.

"Fila looks a lot more advanced in her pregnancy than Daphne does," I noticed. "May be she didn't need the fertility pills at all," I wondered. "May be she was already pregnant. I wonder if such a thing is possible? If that's what's going on then Fila's pregnancy could date back to when I first met her. She might be as much as six months pregnant."

All the way to New York I tried to get Ms. Helmsley interested in her Orange County projects. But she seemed more interested in finishing Dr. Spock's baby book."

"It must be the hormones from pregnancy," I thought. "May be she'll be interested in my teaching her about some of the tantric Buddhist practices," I found myself hoping later as I held my wife's very attractive body close to mine in the generous size first class airplane seat. She had fallen asleep in my arms and was holding me very close. I put the Dr. Spock book in her purse and placed one of the airplane blankets over us. I gently kissed Fila's forehead. "After the baby is born and if she still wants me around," I felt myself hoping.

At the hotel, the clerk handed me a note that Daphne had left for us.

"Daphne's already at the race track," I shouted. Alarm bells went off in my head.

"You don't suppose she's riding that horse, do you Rolf."

"Have these bags sent to our room, will you?" I quickly signed the hotel registry. "And order us a cab, will you." I handed the desk clerk a generous tip.

"Certainly, Mr. Nordquist."

We went right out to the race track and worked our way out to the barns at the back. It had been an unusually hot day and it was still over eighty in the shade. The sun had another couple of hours to go and I was glad Fila had brought a sun hat. "Oh, no," I pointed to one of the jockeys out exercising a horse in the distance. I recognised Rainbow's End and the silouhette of the jockey looked a lot like Daphne's. We rushed over to the practice track.

"You must be Leonard," I put out my hand to the young fellow wearing riding clothes gazing at Rainbow's End. He was scowling out at the horse and rider.

"Rolf and Fila Nordquist," I introduced us. "Daphne's in laws."

"She's out there," Leonard said in a worried tone.

"Trying to find out if Rainbow's End can go the mile and a quarter," he pointed.

Daphne was galloping Rainbow's End quite fast towards the gate. She reined in as she saw us and pulled the big, bay horse up to the gate and rushed over.

"How kind of you to come all this way," Daphne said as she approached us. Fila gave her a big hug. I hugged Daphne as well. I could see Daphne had huge dark circles under her eyes.

"We'll stay for the race," I assured her. Daphne gave us a quick smile and looked vastly relieved.

"How's the horse?" Leonard asked.

"He seems pretty solid, Leonard," Daphne sounded optimistic. "Take him over to the main track, will you? Give him a run and see what you think."

"I know, don't run him full out?" Leonard spoke as Daphne looked like she was going to give him further direction.

She smiled. Leonard let the horse towards the track.

"Is there somewhere we can get out of this sun?" Fila asked.

"We can watch from the stands," Daphne replied. She led the way and after a rather long walk we found ourselves sitting under cover in the grandstand. I went over to the bar and ordered three cold, orange juices.

Daphne took hers and gulped it down. She was concentrating on the track out in front. Leonard and Rainbow's End appeared in a slow gallop rounding the club-house turn and Daphne surveyed the two of them with a worried look on her face.

As Rainbow's End rounded the turn another jockey suddenly pulled his mount up beside him and signalled Leonard he wanted to race. Leonard immediately struck Rainbow's End with his crop and the big horse leaped into a full gallop as both horses tore down the track towards the finish line.

"That's what I mean," Daphne muttered to us, her voice full of dread. "I knew it was a mistake to let Leonard ride Rainbow's End, even if the horse permitted him to mount. Leonard can't refuse a challenge." She watched anxiously as both horses fought furiously for the lead.

"I don't dare let him ride Rainbow's End in the Belmont."

Daphne gave out a long sigh as the horses made it to the finish line in a nose to nose tie.

"Now that's going to start rumors that affect the betting," she sighed.

"You two wait here," Daphne requested. "I've got to go and look at Rainbow's End. His leg might have been injured further by that charge."

I nodded and Daphne rushed off.

"She's much too emotional to make a proper judgement," Fila commented.

"I know, sweetie. We can only hope that horse has it's leg bleeding or some sign of injury. That way Daphne might be forced to scratch it from the race. I don't think she's in her usual state of mind at all."

"Perhaps we should speak to whoever's in charge of the jockeys. May be we should tell them that Daphne is pregnant?"

"No, sweetie," I advised against it. "She'll never forgive us if we interfere that way."

I picked up the emotional charge of the others in the grandstand as we could see Daphne having her discussion with Leonard. The stands were full of trainers, bettors, owners, and other interested parties as the hopefuls for the Belmont took part in their allotted practice runs.

"Everyone is watching Daphne and Leonard," Fila remarked.

"Rainbow's End is one of the favorites for the race, Sweetie. Everyone here has a vested interest in whether the horse is going to run and who is going to ride him."

"Leonard and Daphne look like they're having quite an argument," Fila remarked. I followed her gaze. Leonard suddenly stalked off the field. Daphne grabbed the bridle and led the horse towards the barns at the back. They disappeared out of sight.

"We had better go over there," Fila ordered. "Daphne needs some emotional support. I was trying to get her out of the sun by moving to this grandstand but I guess there's no chance she's going to come back after that scene."

"You sure you can take the sun?" I looked worriedly at Fila.

"This hat does a good job. Don't worry about me."

We found our way over to the space assigned to Rainbow's End and found Daphne bent over the horse's lower leg applying cold water towels to it.

"I told Leonard I wasn't going to let him ride Rainbow's End in the Belmont and he told me he was going to accept an offer to ride one of the other horses in the race," she sobbed.

"Is the horse injured?" I asked softly.

"The leg is slightly swollen. I've asked a vet to come over and take a look at it," Daphne confessed.

"You need to get out of this heat, Daphne," Fila advised. "Your face is bright red."

"You can't leave these horses alone, Fila," Daphne replied. "There's too much at stake. Someone might slip something into their water or food."

"Daphne, you can't stay here night and day," Fila looked horrified. "The race is still several days off."

"I'll stay here," I volunteered. "You go back with Fila to the hotel and cool off a bit in the air conditioning. Just tell me what and when I'm supposed to feed this beast."

"I'll feed him before I go, Rolf. But promise me you won't leave here for a minute. There's a cot at the back."

"I'll position it so I have a full view of the horse, Daphne. Don't worry."

"I'll be back later, Rolf, when it cools off a little. I confess I am feeling a bit faint."

Daphne put out some oats for the horse and some hay in his feeder. Fila led Daphne off.

"Now I'm the babysitter for a racehorse," I sighed as I moved the cot to block the opening to Rainbow's End's stall. "Anyone who want to get to the horse will have to move me first," I decided. I collapsed onto the cot. "Guess it's safe to nod off for a while." I chanted a Buddhist mantra and felt myself falling off to sleep.

I woke up with Fila shaking me awake.

"It's morning already?" I stared at the light in the barn with surprise. I uncoiled myself from the cot and stood up. Daphne went in to check on Rainbow's End.

"His leg is still slightly swollen, Rolf," she advised me. Did that vet come and look at him?"

"No, Daphne. No one came to look at the horse."

"Damn, it's so confused here, with all this activity to do with the Belmont going on. I can see Fila is right. I'm going to scratch Rainbow's End from the race. It's the only humane thing to do. Like Fila says, there are always other races."

"What about Drew, Daphne?"

"He didn't even bother to phone, or leave a message." Daphne told us that she had phoned the house but that Michael had said that Drew hadn't come home last night. She said she hadn't bothered to phone the office.

"The company lawyer says that if you leave Drew it might cause problems for child custody. You might be viewed as the guilty party by the judge."

"I hope the baby is a girl. I don't imagine Drew will even bother to request custody, then."

"What if it's a boy?"

"I'll cross that bridge if I have to. I'm not going to go back to that Newport beachhouse. It holds too many bad memories for me. And I'm not going to remain in a marriage that will cause me to lose all integrity."

"Where will you go, Daphne?" Fila sounded extremely worried.

"I've got friends in Kentucky." Daphne told us that she had already arranged to have Gypsy Strolling sent out to her friend's stables and would have Rainbow's End sent there, too. Daphne said that she had the money from the Derby in her own account and that she would start another training stable up in Kentucky, again.

"I just hope your father doesn't get too upset over this, Fila."

"Father needs to realise the truth about Drew, Daphne. He needs to know how unstable Drew really is."

Daphne went off to pull Rainbow's End out of the race and make some arrangements to ship the horse out to Kentucky. Fila and I sat down on the cot and watched Rainbow's End tie into the hay Daphne put out for him.

"You didn't tell her about the surfboard rental person in Hawaii, did you, sweetie?"

"No, but I think she suspects Drew plays around, Rolf. She had a funny sound in her voice when she discussed how he's always busy in the evenings."

"I wonder if your brother knows what a wonderful lady he's losing?"

"Drew's so immature, Rolf. I think it will be years before Drew will be able to be faithful to one partner. He seems to take his anger at our mother's death and his own failings on members of the opposite sex. He may need professional help or something."

"May be that explains some of his impulsivity and problems with anger control."

"Tell Daphne not to contact Drew until she's safely located with both race horses and herself back in Kentucky, Fila. He's likely to be furious when he realises she's not coming back."

"Not to mention what father will do."

CHAPTER 17.

The Unexpected.

Fila and I stayed in New York for a couple of days. It took that long to have Rainbow's End shipped safely to Kentucky. Once he and Daphne were safely aboard planes to Kentucky, Fila and I took the first flight we could get back to California.

"Thank goodness the swelling on Rainbow's End's leg finally went down," I remarked to Ms. Helmsley as we flew across the country in the first class section of a Boeing 767. "I think Daphne was more worried about that horse than she was about whatever Drew is going to do once he hears she's left him and moved her stable back to Kentucky."

"I'm worried about Daphne, Rolf. She's much too intense for the final months of pregnancy. Not to mention much too active. I don't think all this worry and activity is good for her."

"I know, sweetie. Imagine Drew not even attempting to contact her here, even after he turned up at the office and your father chewed him out. Whatever can he be thinking?"

"We'll find out soon." Fila sounded grim. "Daphne's already faxed him a letter requesting a legal separation. She got a lawyer from Kentucky who's an old friend of the family to draft the letter. And father's furious. He's talking about changing his will again."

We landed in Los Angeles that evening and drove down to Newport beach in a rental car. I headed for the coffee pot in the executive lounge of Enderby Developments the next morning. I hadn't had much sleep, just kept rolling around dreading what Drew would do once he got Daphne's letter.

"He might have it already," I realized. Fila had said something about it being faxed. I got halfway down the hall carrying my coffee cup when Alvin came running up to me.

"Rolf, Geoffrey wants you in his office, immediately. Something to do with Drew, I think."

I went down to Enderby's office. As Lucille let me into his area I was shocked to see Drew sitting in one of Enderby's chairs. He looked shell-shocked.

"Nordquist," Drew yelled at me. "We need to talk."

"May be you can think of something to help this situation, Rolf," Enderby said, his voice ominously quiet.

"What situation?" I asked Drew.

"I've told Drew to go to Kentucky and beg Daphne to come back and he refuses," Enderby said wearily. "Says he's not going to give up his mistress for anything."

"His mistress?" I freaked.

"Daphne must have found out about my affair with Linda, Nordquist." Drew told me that Daphne's lawyer had sent him a letter from Kentucky demanding a legal separation, and that I had to do something to get custody of the kid for him, once it was born.

"Your affair with Linda," I gasped. "Which Linda?" I managed. "Not Linda Wright, I hope." I couldn't believe my ears. Linda Wright was the talented administrative assistant Geoffrey had personally assigned to Drew to smooth out his business interactions when I had insisted we give him more responsibility. She was a very attractive lady almost old enough to be Drew's mother.

"Surely you know about it," Drew questioned my look of complete disbelief. "Linda is somewhat older than me but everyone suspected, I'm sure. We were always alone together in my office late into the evening."

"No, I didn't know about it, Drew," I tried to keep my voice calm. "What exactly do you want me to do? Shouldn't I try and find out if Daphne might be willing to come back to you. Perhaps, some marital conselling would help? How did she find out about Linda?"

"I don't know, Nordquist, but Daphne must know all right. Otherwise, nothing in this world would convince her to leave me, particularly with our baby's birth so near. Daphne is absolutely dotty about me. Always has been since I met her in Kentucky."

"Has anything else happened lately, Drew? May be there's some other reason Daphne left you?" I couldn't believe Drew's words. I realized he was in complete denial about what had really caused Daphne to give up on him.

"Oh, well, we did have an argument over that stupid race horse of hers, you know, Rainbow's End. And I didn't go to the Belmont with her. But I'm sure that's not what caused Daphne to send me that letter. Someone in this office must have told her about Linda."

"Where is Daphne, now, Drew?" I asked patiently like I didn't know.

"In Kentucky, of all places, Nordquist." Drew told me that Daphne had withdrawn Rainbow's End from the Belmont, spirited her other horse, Gypsy Strolling, out of their stable and was now saying that she was setting up another stable in her own name in Kentucky. Drew said that it had to be revenge for his affair with Linda Wright and he didn't know what to do.

"You need to go to Kentucky, yourself, Drew, and see if you can apologize and talk things over with Daphne, like your father says."

"Enderbys never apologise, Nordquist!" Drew replied. He asked if I hadn't found that out yet with his sister? He said he was bored with Daphne, as all she was interested in was racehorses and stated that he was not going to give up Linda. He said he found her fascinating and that she and him made the perfect couple. He said that outside of myself, Linda was the only person who had ever validated his business talent, and he didn't know how he could do without her at the office. He told me that Linda advised him what to say to the military oafs he had to deal with in the several projects that his father had assigned to him.

"What does Linda think you should do about Daphne, Drew?" I asked.

"She says to let Daphne go if she wants out", he replied. Drew told me that I needed to find a way to get Daphne to give up her rights to the kid once it was born, as after all, Linda had told him that I had a responsibility to Enderby Developments, being its interim CEO and all.

I reeled. This is what it's going to be like when Geoffrey dies, I thought. Drew and Linda Wright are going to think they can order me around.

I glanced at Enderby.

"You do the mediation over this, Rolf," he ordered. "I'm feeling rather tired. I think I'll go home shortly."

I could see Drew's behavior had hit him hard. I decided to try and protect Daphne.

"Women never do that, Drew, give up the right to their kids," I told him. I advised him that he would have to settle for partial custody, particularly as he was the guilty party and his affair with Linda Wright made it sound like he was. I told him that partial custody consisted of visitation rights and some kind of input into the baby's upbringing and education, particularly if the baby was a boy and was going to inherit Enderby Developments' controlling stock when he was of age. I told Drew that he would need to make sure the child was given the best of a business education.

I tried to get the best deal I could for Daphne. I knew all she cared about now was keeping primary custody of her unborn child. Drew seemed to take seriously what I had said. He stayed quiet for a long time.

"You want me to have company lawyers draw up something like that in an agreement for you, Drew? What's Daphne demanding in settlement? Half your assets, I imagine?"

"No, oddly enough, Nordquist, she isn't demanding anything except her two race horses and the money from the Derby. I think she's entitled to that under our pre-nuptial agreement anyway."

"I'll try to convince Daphne she shouldn't press for full custody, Drew." I told him how judges are if you had to go through the courts and how they almost always gave the benefit to the wife

if adultery could be proven. I told him that the judge would probably hold him to some kind of childcare allowance based on his
income once the baby was born, and likely, alimony for Daphne,
too. I told him that those allowances could get unbelievably expensive.

Drew blanched.

"OK, Nordquist, draw up the agreement. I'll go see what Linda
thinks. See what you can do. I'm going to take a few weeks off. I
want to show Linda the sights of Honolulu. The surfing there is
terrific this time of year. Eight feet and higher surfs right in Waikiki."

"Drop by in an hour, Drew, after you've talked to Linda and
before you go. I'll have the company lawyers draft an offer. They'll
need your signature. I'll fly right out to Kentucky and see if I can
persuade Daphne to go along with the agreement."

"Thanks, Nordquist," he said. "You know, you're really not
the louse I thought you were when I first met you. At least you
recognize that I have business talent. And I can see that you're
willing to go that extra mile for Linda and I. I like that in an
employee."

Drew glared at his father and rushed out the door.

"That sound reasonable, Geoffrey?" I asked.

"I'd rather have Daphne as my grandson's guardian, Rolf, rather
than that ass of a son I have. See what you can do. I'm going to go
back to the beach house and lie down."

What a fortuitous set of circumstances for Daphne, I thought
as I rushed over to the lawyers' wing. I shook my head at Linda
Wright's betrayal of the responsibility Geoffrey had given her.

Drew and Linda make a perfect pair, I thought. Neither of
them can be trusted. I wonder how long Drew will be infatuated
with that lady? Until she feels confident enought to criticize or
disagree with him, I imagine.

CHAPTER 18.

Rapid Changes.

A month after I flew out to Kentucky and got Daphne to agree to a separation giving partial custody of her child to Drew, I got a panic call from Fila at the office.

"Daphne's gone into premature labor, Rolf. And she's only a little over six months pregnant. I'm really worried about her."

"Throw some clothes together, sweetie. I'll get tickets on the next flight to Kentucky."

When we got to the hospital the receptionist told us that Daphne had already given birth to a three pound four ounce baby boy two hours before. Fila sat down on one of the chairs in the lobby for a moment. Then both of us rushed to the window of the intensive care nursery. Daphne's baby was visible, sleeping soundly inside it's specially equipped crib. He was being fed intravenously and other wires were attached but the baby looked contented enough. We found Daphne's room. She waved wearily at us. Fila rushed over and gave her a big hug. I transferred the two dozen red roses we had picked up on the way into a large vase and placed them onto the end table next to Daphne's bed.

"The baby look's fine," Fila reassured Daphne. I was enormously proud of my wife. Her voice betrayed nothing except happiness for Daphne. She gave no sign of reaction to her loss of multi-million dollars of assets and any chance of being CEO of Enderby Developments.

"I know," Daphne beamed. "He's small but the doctor says he's not expecting any complications from the early birth. I've named him Oliver Rolf Enderby after my father and you Rolf. I want you to be the baby's godfather."

I nodded, smiled and gave her a big hug.

"Are you all right, Daphne?" Fila inquired.

"I'm tired, Fila and saddened by my poor judgement for a father of my child. I had Drew contacted but some administrative assistant of his told my contact that Drew is too busy to come out and view the baby at this time."

"I can't believe that, Daphne," Fila gasped.

"It's probably for the best" I advised. "The less Drew sees of the boy the more secure your guardianship of him will remain."

"I'm so happy at Oliver's birth," she beamed. "And it was so good of you two to come all the way out here so fast."

"I had to take a look at my first nephew," Fila laughed.

"You really don't mind that I've had a boy ahead of you, do you Fila?"

"Of course not, sweetie," Fila assured her.

"I'm sorry, Fila. I really hope Oliver grows up and doesn't want to become involved in Enderby Developments."

"I know. After what you've been through no one would expect you to think otherwise. But don't think that far ahead. For all you know, Oliver could take after you and want to be a horse trainer or a jockey. At least with you as his mother, he'll have a choice in the matter. Just let him follow his heart. He'll know what to do."

I couldn't believe Fila's words.

"It must be Zot's influence," I decided, looking at my wife with intense pleasure. It was like she was a changed personality.

"How is your father, Fila? I was afraid that my breakup with Drew would cause further deterioration in his condition."

"Father's not good at all. But don't blame yourself. Father said to give you his love and his gratitude for providing a grandson. He would have flown out here if he could have but there is just no way. Father is bedridden. The company doctor has nurses by his side around the clock now. The only thing that deadens his pain is steady, intravenous morphine."

"How sad," Daphne sighed.

"Rolf, what are you going to do now? You're not going to put up with Drew's arrogance after Geoffrey's death are you, and stay on as interim chief executive officer of Enderby Developments?"

"Only as long as it takes to set up a board of trustees to run the company." I felt relief go through every bone of my body.

"That's enough celebrating for now!" Daphne's doctor had come into the room.

"This young lady requires rest," he ordered.

"We'll be back tomorrow, Daphne," I promised. I could tell by the dark circles under her eyes that the doctor was quite correct. She smiled gratefully, hugged Fila and waved goodbye.

Fila and I wound our way out of the hospital and into our rental car.

We'll have to give Father, Lama Tsot and Alvin a call, Rolf," Fila advised. "They will be thrilled to hear everything is all right."

"Are you sure you're not terribly upset by Oliver's birth, sweetie?"

"Of course I am. I'm happy for Daphne but I feel devastated. All of father's work, and that of his father before him, to make Enderby Developments what it is today. I can't believe I won't have a hand in drafting it's future. According to the terms of father's will it's Drew that will inherit the controlling shares of Enderby Developments now."

"Think of names of possible trustees you think can continue with the company's success, sweetie. I'll give their names to the board when your father goes. May be strong trustees can counteract whatever influence Drew can bring to play."

"Good idea. I can think of several strong people right off the top of my head."

"Just make sure they believe in social responsibility as well as profit, sweetie. That way, Enderby Developments might be a force for good in the world."

"All right. I'll keep that advice in mind."

"You've changed, sweetie. Whatever's happened to, Miss Helmsley," I told her, taking her into my arms. I kissed her tenderly as I could feel her shaking violently.

Fila managed a wan smile as I released her.

"We need to get Oliver a present, Rolf. What do you think if we check out that big baby furniture warehouse we saw from the freeway. I think we should get him his first horse, you know, one of those wooden rocking horses."

"Sounds like a good idea to me. Right after we settle into a motel."

CHAPTER 19.

Change Of Leadership.

God, it's hard to die, I swore as I endured one of my more lucid episodes between long periods of unconsciousness when the morphine knocked me right out. Anger surged through me as I felt the intense pain that had become ubiquitous during my every waking moment. I surveyed the only place I had left to me now that the unspeakable horror that had struck me was eating away my lungs, my bedroom. My eyes fixated on the wedding pictures of Fila and Rolf as well as Daphne and Drew. They were displayed within my view on my expensive, koa dresser.

"At least, Rolf and Fila's marriage has worked out," I thought. I tried to dull my pain as I thought of Drew's and Daphne's. Drew will be surprised, I mused, by the change in my will.

I looked at as much of my lush, tropical garden as I could see through the window with longing. If only I could nurture my rare orchid plants one last time. My eyes returned to the family portrait.

At least, I still look like one of the living in that marriage portrait, I congratulated myself on how well I had hidden the ravages of my disease using make up for so long. But once Daphne provided an heir to Enderby Developments I no longer had to force myself to go to the office. I've got Rolf to run the company until Daphne's son Oliver is old enough to take over, I realized. I could just give in to my rage about Drew's behavior and my unexpected and horrible death.

With Fila married to a man capable of running Enderby Resources, I mused, I thought it would be easy to let go and just cease to exist. But it's not, damn it. I just continue to go on suffering in unbearable pain.

God knows I'm not needed any longer to keep the company on an even keel. Rolf does it very well. Why is my physical body putting up such a fight anyway? God knows my mind is more than willing to throw in the towel.

Fierce pain gripped my lungs in an iron vice.

Is this really necessary? I mentally shouted at my body. Can't you just cease to exist, you wasted piece of flesh? The pain was unbearable when I was awake. Like someone was jabbing me in the chest with long, thin knives that tormented but didn't kill.

And I can't bear the sensation of drowning in my own lung fluids. It's ghastly.

There must be some way to end this suffering, I cursed. Maybe if I asked Fila she would arrange an assisted suicide. The idea appealed immensely as another severe coughing attack struck. I was helpless to stem the blood flow when that happened. The salty tasting blood flowed out my mouth and soaked the elegant cover on my bed.

It isn't fair, I cursed. Animals they put out of their suffering, humans they torment.

"You poor soul," one of the ever changing nurses that the company doctor had arranged came charging into the room in response to my coughing. I cringed at her pity. I hadn't wasted much pity to those down on their luck throughout my life and I didn't want any for myself now. The nurse held absorbent cloths to my mouth and held me from shaking furiously until finally the unbearable burning sensation in my lungs ended and my current episode was over. Rage filled me again as the nurse attached more plasma to the intravenous drip system in my arm that kept me from ceasing to exist.

"Don't," I gasped, trying desperately to speak. "You're just prolonging my agony," I could hardly understand the sounds my mouth was making.

"It's the doctor's orders, I'm sorry," the middle-aged nurse replied. I could feel even more of her pity as she mopped up the blood on my face and changed the bed covers.

I mentally let loose a stream of curses at the nurse and the entire medical profession.

If they pity you so much, why the hell don't they end your suffering? I thought. The nurse got ready to give me another shot of the morphine that I knew would send me off into unconsciousness again. I couldn't wait.

If only I would stay out permanently.

"Mr. Enderby, Rolf say you want speak Lama Tsot?" I looked up. Lama Tsot had come into the room.

That didn't take long, I thought. It was just this morning I asked Rolf to have Lama Tsot pay a visit.

The nurse gave Lama Tsot, his orange and red robe, and his shaved head a look of complete disbelief. I waved the welcome shot of morphine off.

"Not now," I managed. "I want to speak to the Lama."

"If you insist, Mr. Enderby." The nurse looked disaprovingly at both of us.

"Be quick about it, whoever you are," she ordered the Lama. "He's in great pain."

"No talk Mr. Enderby," Lama Tsot ordered. He seemed to sense how painful it was for me to do so.

"I need help to kill myself," I gasped. "Will you ask Fila to arrange it?"

Lama Tsot looked shocked and shook his head.

Damn, I cursed. I should have done something myself sooner. But the deterioration came too quickly for me.

"No do dat, Mr. Enderby," Lama Tsot spoke firmly. "Or ask someone else do for you. Bad karma. Cause very bad re-birth. Come back animal realm, maybe even insect realm. Or go direct 'hell realm' or maybe 'hungry ghost realm' where wander hungry, tirsty, long fo food, water, but only have tiny mouth, can never get enuff. You tink suffer here. Dere suffering magnified hundred, ten tousand time."

Rage filled me. Even if the Lama had won the Kentucky Derby he was like many professionals, doctors, clergymen, and nurses, indifferent when the chips were down.

"Forgive me for asking!" I waved the Lama to leave. Instead, he drew up a chair and sat down.

"Pain different fo Buddhists," he explained, signalling me not to try to talk. "In Buddhism, suffering signal fo practice, not try avoid like in west."

"Practice?" I gasped.

"Wen pain strike, Buddhist practitioner sense opportunity."

"Opportunity?" I said with disbelief. "Opportunity for what for God's sake? To try and be heroic. I just need to cease to exist."

"Wat you ask, 'cease to exist,' not possible, Mr. Enderby. One ting sentient beings can not do. No 'cease to exist.' Consciousness go on. Wat you call natural law. Even when die, go on. Den need try go Bardos."

"Damn," I cursed. "Go away. I don't want to hear this. The last thing I want to do is keep on in this state."

"Not be dis state," the Lama seemed amused. "Have leave body behind when die. Only mind, Buddha nature go on. But you no try talk. Lama Tsot explain." The Lama put his first finger to his lips. I tried to ignore my rage, and the searing pain in my chest. I was forced to listen to what he was saying.

"Important you know somting before die, Mr. Enderby. All life you always angry, critical self, wife, children, employees. You blame, imtimidate, censor, treaten instead empower dem."

"Damn you, go away," I tried to call the nurse back but wound up choking up blood instead.

"You see," the Lama wiped the blood from my mouth. "Anger no work. You die soon. State mind important wen die. Not want be angry. Not want be in fear. Not want even be anxious. Wen die mind all powerful. Anger, fear magnified many time. Mind play tricks after dead. Perceive wrong. Tink water boiling oil. Tink field wasteland. Easy make mistake."

I had no choice but to listen. I couldn't shut out the Lama's voice.

"Need be calm, need realise mind play tricks or you have terrifying experiences. Wen moment of death opportunity dat Buddhist study dis life all time fo happen. Dey try recognize true nature of mind. Called Buddha Nature. You 'part of God,' Mr. Enderby. Moment of death, possible recognize true nature of mind. Go direct enlightenment. Nirvana. It possible."

"Part of God," what nonsense, I thought. Where is one of those bloody nurses when you need them?

"If not recognize Buddha Nature at death, sentient being go sleep tree days." Lama Tsot's voice carried on with information I neither wanted nor believed.

"If not recognize true nature mind at moment of death den need try reach Bardos, Mr. Enderby. Have goal in mind when die. Or might get lost, can be trapped here. Sometime people cling possessions. Try comfort relatives. Not good. Tink you need help transfer consciousness to Bardos when die. Lama Tsot help, come wen he tink you dying, promise."

May be he'll go away if I look like I'm understanding what he's talking about, I thought. I nodded in agreement.

"Also wen make Bardos, not want react happingings dere. Wrathful deities come. Non-Buddhists tink dey be monsters. Be very afraid. Try seek rapid rebirth. Result very bad re-birth. Wrathful deities not monsters. Only wat you call active principle in universe. Try not be afraid."

Sure, I nodded my head like I was believing him.

"Bout pain, suffering, Mr. Enderby. Disease opportunity do 'Tong-Len' practice. Take on pain all sentient beings suffering from same disease. Ease dere suffering. Just try relax mind, take on all pain sufferers everyware wit lung cancer. Lama Tsot do same, den consciousness go Buddha fields as we do Phowa. You try."

That's preposterous, I thought with even more anger. My lungs were burning up with pain. Why did I think this joker might be willing to help? I willed a nurse to return with my shot of morphine. But the Lama had closed his eyes. He was seated in front of me and was chanting something in Tibetan.

I'll have to look like I'm trying to follow him, I decided. Or he'll never go away. I closed my eyes and tried to look like I was listening.

"Breadth in," he ordered. "Take on suffering all sentient beings," he explained in his broken English. "Breadth out, transfer pain to Buddha Fields. You see."

What the Hell are Buddha fields? I cursed.

"Follow Lama Tsot," he ordered. I was so anxious to look like I was following him so he would go away that I tried taking a deep breath in when he did. My lungs fiercely protested as they were forced to expand in their diseased state.

"Imagine udders suffering like you," Lama Tsot spoke.

God, I can see them in my mind, I realised with horror. Visions of people in hospitals were coming into my mind. Men and women alike in various states of lung cancer. Some were like me, hooked to intravenous tubes. Some were in hospital chairs desperately trying to suck in some nicotine from lit cigarettes despite their illness. Others were almost comatose. It looked like some of them had one of their lungs surgically removed. Their bed coverings sagged on one side. Most were screaming in pain but no nurse was running to their help. I could even see some people dying painfully in their own beds at home. I guessed they were without medical insurance.

"Feel dere pain," Lama Tsot commanded. I joined him in a deep in-breath again. My body shuddered. I groaned aloud as my pain intensified one-hundred fold. I stared at the faces in my head. One of the women screamed, her pain was so bad. I pitied her.

"Good," I heard the Lama's voice through a haze of pain. "You feel compassion. Now breadth out and transfer pain Buddha Fields."

I gave a long sigh as I exhaled. The pain seemed to lessen a bit.

Must be some kind of hypnotism, I decided. But who cares as long as he goes away.

"Breadth in suffering," Lama Tsot told me. I took another deep breath. Intense pain racked my body again. I groaned loudly.

"Breathe out pain. Transfer consciousness Buddha fields." I exhaled desperately. I could feel the pain lessen again. I looked at the Lama, this time in surprise.

"You help udders, dere pain better now," Lama Tsot assured me. I looked at the tortured faces in my mind. My God, they are resting easier now, I realised.

I followed the Lama's lead for several minutes. His crazy instructions were somehow easing my pain. Everyone's pain seemed to be getting less and less. My own lungs felt more like they had done in the past.

"Dat enuff for now," Lama Tsot told me as my nurse came back into the room. "You practice," he ordered. "Not much time left fo you."

"Lama Tsot come back later Mr. Enderby," he said as the nurse inserted yet another needle into my arm. I tried to protest but I was too weak from all the breathing practice.

How did he do that? I thought of the pictures I had seen in my mind as the morphine started to knock me out. Must be the power of suggestion.

"Call me wen Mr. Enderby wakes up again," I heard Lama Tsot instruct the nurse.

"What's he want with the likes of you?" she queried.

"Tink Mr. Enderby going die soon." the Lama told the nurse. Lama Tsot come, do 'Phowa,' help transfer consciousness to Buddha fields."

"Buddha fields, oh, you're a Buddist Lama, eh, like that one that won the Kentucky Derby. What's a rich and successful Christian man like Mr. Enderby doing with a Buddhist Lama?"

"Mr. Enderby dying," the Lama repeated. "Lama Tsot clergyman."

"If you ask me, if he's dying, he would be better off with a Christian minister, not a heathen like you. But nobody ever asks me, anyway," she complained.

Thank God, I mentally celebrated the nearness of death.

"And you're wrong, the doctor says he's got another few weeks at the earliest," the nurse argued.

When I awoke enough to orient myself later Lama Tsot was sitting beside me on a chair. Rolf, Fila, and Drew were with him. I felt extremely weak.

It must be night, I mused. The room seemed dim and gloomy. Why don't they turn a light on, I thought.

"God, father really is dying," Drew spoke, shock in his voice. "Now we'll see who's going to be the head of Enderby Developments Nordquist! I asked Father to change his will to give me control."

Fila gasped.

"Dis no time argue," Lama Tsot spoke sharply.

"Important dat dying person be able leave witout tinking tings not been taken care, left undone. Dey no need hear son, daughter fight fo control or udders fight over belongings."

"Lama Tsot is right Drew." Fila spoke as harshly to her brother as the Lama. "Say your final goodbyes to Father."

"You've taken care of everything, Father," Fila spoke. "Don't feel you have to hang on. We know you're in great pain."

Tears came to my eyes. "At least Fila understands," I thought warmly of my daughter.

"Thanks, Fila," I muttered. I could hardly hear my own voice. Fila came closer and leaned over me kissing me on the forehead.

"Thanks for helping with the company, Fila," I gasped. "After your mother died. You were a great help." I gazed at my daughter. Tears filled her eyes.

"Don't try and talk, Father."

I felt myself want to say goodbye to Drew.

"Drew," I managed. He came over and leaned over the bed. I looked at my son. I couldn't see him clearly. My vision seemed to be failing.

"I can hear you Father," Drew's voice had anger in it.

"You're so like me," I whispered. "So much anger." Drew didn't answer.

"Give Rolf a hand, will you?" I asked. "With the business."

"Geoffrey wants you to handle some more of the important out-of-state projects," Rolf told Drew. I managed a slight smile.

"Good for you Rolf," I thought. "Always diplomatic." I hadn't said anything to him about Drew handling any more projects.

"He does?" Drew's eyes suddenly filled with tears. "May be that's how he is going to give me more control."

The Lama came near and felt my pulse.

"Lama Tsot tink end near," he said quietly.

"For God's sake," Fila started crying openly.

"No try talk," the Lama warned me.

"Signs all say it time, Mr. Enderby," he advised. "You dying now. Must be calm. Remember no anger, no fear, no sadness. Opportunity fo you recognize true nature mind, reach Nirvana," Fila's sobs increased.

"If not take opportunity recognize true nature of mind den give intent go Bardos as die. Important. No try hang on belongings. All taken care of."

Just let me go? I begged mentally, somehow annoyed by my daughter's tears. I'm more than ready to go, believe me.

"Try not cry," Lama Tsot instructed Fila. Rolf put his arms around her.

"Relatives cry, hold person back from go Bardos," he warned Fila. Her sobs lessened. I felt relieved.

"It's so dark in here," I complained.

"Sight go, Mr. Enderby," Lama Tsot advised. I could hardly hear what he was saying.

"Do 'Tong-Len'," he commanded. "Like befo. Lama Tsot help."

"In breadth, take on pain of udder lung cancer victims."

Instinctively, I obeyed. I tried to inhale. Severe pain stabbed me in the chest. I couldn't see Lama Tsot or anyone else in the room but suddenly visions of lung cancer sufferers filled my mind. Their suffering was enormous. My body shuddered at the enormity of their suffering.

"Now breadth out," Lama Tsot's voice was faint but it was still reaching me.

I released my breath. All I managed was a gasp.

"But the doctor said he had at least another several weeks," Fila protested.

"Breadth in," Lama Tsot commanded. I managed another tortured breath. A vision of a man screaming filled my mind. It looked like he was in a coma but he was still screaming in pain. A stabbing sensation hit me in my lungs. It felt like someone was stabbing me with a red hot sword.

"No give in fear, breadth out," Lama Tsot commanded. "Go Buddha fields," I gasped out. The pain lessened slightly. The man in the bed in a coma stopped screaming.

"One more time," Lama Tsot commanded. My lungs felt like they were collapsing. I gagged. Suddenly I couldn't hear the Lama's voice anymore. I knew I had to breathe out one more time. I managed a long sigh, then darkness seemed to be all around me. Somehow I knew I was going. Blackness filled everything. I couldn't breathe in again.

"Your fadder gone," Lama Tsot said to Fila. "Now we do Phowa. Guide to Bardos." It was the last thing I heard.

CHAPTER 20.

Aftermath.

I felt like the weight of the world was on my shoulders. Fila, Drew, Alvin and I were in a small room for the reading of Geoffrey Enderby's will. All I wanted to do was go back to my old way of life and Fila was begging me to hang in here until even after our child was born.

"What a scene we had the night Enderby died," I remembered. Fila was overcome with grief and anxiety.

"Rolf, you can't leave me now. You're all I've got."

I went into shock. I stepped away from Fila. I had been cradling her in my arms.

"That wasn't the deal, Ms. Helmsley," I said softly. I was completely surprised. My rich, beautiful lady seemed to hold me in more regard than I had thought.

"At least, stay on until the baby is born, Rolf?" she begged. I picked up her intense anxiety.

"Fila, that's not for another three months," I said softly. "My CD is ready to distribute. I have to push it in person, do some live concerts. Otherwise, the CD is just going to be totally ignored."

"I'll pay you whatever the CD could be expected to bring in, Rolf. And if you'll stay on just for a few months after our baby's birth I'll guarantee you a yearly allowance for life." Fila dissolved into sobs. I had never seen her so desperate.

I had never before felt so trapped. Then it got worse. I looked at Fila's growing waistline. The baby was showing. I was suddenly overcome with a feeling of responsibility for my unborn child. I sensed that Fila's desperate emotional state was not good for the baby. I put my arms around her again.

"Just relax, Ms. Helmsley," I tried to lighten her mood. "Heavy emotion isn't good for the fetus," I warned her.

"Just say you'll stay on for another few months after the baby is born, Rolf," Fila begged. "It's going to take that long to settle who's in control of Enderby Developments. I can feel it. Drew is going to fight the setting up of a board of trustees, I know he is. He's going to threaten a legal challenge unless the directors let him manage the company for his son."

I realised that Fila wasn't thinking of our unborn child. She was still consumed with business matters. I sensed I needed to do something preventive for our child. A bargain came into my head.

"Fila, I'm not interested in money but I care about our unborn child. If I stay on as CEO past the baby's birth like you want, will you let me have some kind of custody of the child?"

Miss Helmsley pulled out of my arms.

"That wasn't the deal, Rolf. What happened to Mr. I don't want any attachment in my life?"

We both stared at each other in surprise. I couldn't believe my own words. It was as if the soul of the unborn baby was invading me or something.

"Don't leave me alone here, Daddy," I could sense it saying. "I don't want to become like Mommy or Uncle Drew."

"Does it matter, Ms. Helmsley? Do we have a deal?"

Fila pondered my offer in her mind for the longest time.

"Not full custody, Rolf. Partial access, may be, and I won't have the father of my child begging on Laguna Beach again, you'll have to accept some kind of yearly income."

"Joint custody?" I insisted.

We stared at each other for a while.

"All right Rolf," Fila folded.

"You'll have the papers drawn up?"

"Yes, of course."

"It's going to be all right, sweetie," I assured her. She allowed me to hold her in my arms again. I kissed her forehead.

My mind came back to the present. Enderby's head lawyer came into the room.

Drew's words just before his father died struck me.

"I asked Father to change his will to give me more control," he had said.

God, I hope he has, my spirit rose at the thought. It was taking me 16 hours a day to run Enderby Developments. I hated dealing with the military contracts. I had no time for anything else and my CD producer was giving me hell because I told him to put off its release for at least another three months.

What's happened to me? I mused. I find myself waking up at night and worrying about what's going to happen to Fila, I realised. Sometimes I feel that the last thing in the world I want to do is walk away from her. I never should have agreed to her proposition in the first place. We've both changed somehow.

I stopped my musing as Enderby's lawyer sat down behind the huge desk in the room. All of us stared at each other as we realised we would finally know just what the old boy had put into his will. You could have heard a pin drop in the room as the rather grave, older fellow sat down and pulled out an official looking document.

"My condolences about your father," he spoke to Fila and Drew. "He was one of my closest friends."

"Just proceed with the reading of the will," Drew ordered. Anxiety was evident in his voice.

The lawyer cleared his throat and picked up the document. All of us concentrated as he read off the disposition of Enderby's assets. It was fascinating.

Enderby had divided up his worldly goods except his Enderby Developments shares exactly in half. He left the family home in the Newport hills to Drew and the Newport Beach House to Fila. He left his limo and his sports car collection to Drew but he gave his luxury sedan collection to Fila. He divided his other stock and bond holdings exactly in half. I realised that neither Fila nor Drew would ever suffer for money in their lives. Then the lawyer turned to the matter of intense interest to those of us in the room, the controlling shares of Enderby Developments, the ones that were not floating on the public stock market.

"He's changed his will, the bastard," Drew was the first to react. I reeled as the lawyer's words sank in.

"How diabolical, darling," Alvin put his arms around Fila. She too was reeling from the change in the will.

Enderby had left his controlling, 51 percent, stock interest in trust for his first grandson, Oliver, when he reached 21. Not to either his son or daughter as expected. I realised the rules of the game had been changed.

"This is with the understanding that my son-in-law, Rolf Nordquist, remain as chief executive officer of Enderby Developments, with sole decision-making responsibility, at a salary commiserate with such a responsibility, until my first grandson is capable of assuming command. In lieu of Rolf Nordquist's death, a private trust is to be set up with the best of qualified professionals available governing Enderby Developments until my grandson is of age."

My God, now I have to die to escape Enderby Developments, I reeled. I felt like I was trapped for the next 20 years into a guilded prison from which I could do nothing that I wanted to do with my life. But then I thought of Fila's final promise when I accepted her offer the night her father died.

"You'll be free to go immediately, Rolf, I assure you, if you wish, once the board of trustees is set up. No one would expect you to build up assets for Drew. I wouldn't even do it myself if he asked me."

I imagine Miss Helmsley would feel the same about my staying on as CEO until Drew's son was old enough for his inheritance. She would still want me to be free, I thought.

With any luck all I'll need to serve is a month at the most, I thought.

Fila's request had sounded so reasonable the night of her father's death. Only a further three month's delay at the most. "I'll donate to your South American Trust whatever your CD could be expected to bring in, Rolf," she promised. "And I'll guarantee in writing an annual allowance of $100,000 as long as you live. Plus joint custody of our child."

How could I refuse? Only now I was personally hung up with responsibility for my unborn child. And I was even worried about what was going to happen to Fila.

"Mr. Nordquist, the board of directors is waiting for you to set direction." I looked up. It was Enderby's lawyer.

"Just give me a few minutes with Drew," I requested. I went over to Enderby's son. He was deep in conversation with Linda Wright.

"Father's betrayed me again," I heard. "I asked father to give me more control and he didn't listen. Now all I can hope for is the day that my son gets control of Enderby Developments controlling shares."

"Drew, Geoffrey asked me to get you to take charge of all the military projects," I informed him. I ignored Fila frantically shaking her head.

"The military projects, Nordquist?" Some of Drew's anger left him. "Why that's the majority of the out-of-state business."

"That's right, Drew. I would appreciate your overseeing as many of those projects as you are willing to take on."

"I'll come by your office tomorrow, Nordquist," he promised. "This will is not what I wanted but I had better protect my future son's assets, at least."

"You're sure my father asked you that?"

"Yes, Drew, I'm sure," I lied. Linda Wright looked at me oddly.

"Why did you do that, Rolf?" Fila growled at me as Drew and Linda left the room. "You know Drew hasn't any business sense."

"I'm trying to avoid the legal challenge you're worried about, sweetie. Do you realise what a lawsuit on his part might do to setting up a board of trustees? Besides, what can you do to ruin a military project? Every step of the procedure is carefully spelled out."

"May be you're right, Rolf," Fila relented. She accompanied me to the board room.

"I assume you're going to allow me to oversee at least the Orange County projects again?"

"Of course, Miss Helmsley," I assured her.

"I'll fill you in on what's taken place since your father put me in charge of those projects this afternoon, I promise."

"Mr. Nordquist?" I looked up. Enderby's lawyer was handing me a large, sealed envelope.

"Geoffrey instructed me to give you this envelope after his death." He sat down across the table and I opened the envelope. The room was filling up with Enderby Developments directors. I opened up the envelope. There was a short letter and another envelope in it. Fila and Alvin looked at their contents with great curiosity. The first one was in Enderby's handwriting. I read it.

> "Rolf, you'll have to forgive me for butting into your personal life. When I realised from a private investigator's report that you were the son of Johan Nordquist of Nordquist Insurance of Baltimore, I took the liberty of informing him of your marriage to Fila."

My heart pounded.

> "He sent me this letter to give to you after my death. I don't know it's contents but I hope it helps you settle your family problems. I told your father that you have too much management talent to be left out of the future of his business."

I gasped. My God. Enderby wasn't just satisfied with tying me down with his business responsibilities for life, he also wanted me to go back to carrying the weight of my father's business. My head was reeling. I tore open the other envelope. I nearly fainted as I recognized my own father's handwriting.

"Rolf," I read.

"Delighted that you have finally decided to return to the world of business rather than that nonsensical devotion to the exotic religion you seemed to be obsessed with. I would have thought that you would have had the decency to inform your mother and I of your marriage plans, but perhaps that was too much to expect after 15 years of silence. Your mother insists we come out to Newport Beach and meet your new wife. It's against my better judgement but to put her mind at ease you can expect us at your doorstep after Geoffrey Enderby's funeral."

Sincerely,
Johan Nordquist.

My mind shot into some kind of whirling vortex. Enderby's funeral had already taken place. That meant my parents might be at Fila's door any moment. I somehow managed to get through my first meeting as Enderby's chosen replacement by babbling something about continuing on with my present style of leadership.

"I've got to find Zot," I vowed as I rushed out of the office. Fila grabbed on to my arm as I stumbled down the hallway.

"What was in that envelope, Rolf?" she demanded. "It threw you into orbit." I handed her and Alvin both notes as we ducked into Enderby's office.

"My God!" she gasped, as she read the contents.

"How diabolical," Alvin commented.

"I can't believe my father did that," Fila was in shock. "No wonder you're upset. What are you going to do?"

"I've got to go find Zot, Fila," I stammered. "The last thing I wanted in my life was for my father to know my whereabouts again. Do you mind if we put off that briefing on the Orange County projects? I promise I'll do it tonight after I get back from Zot's."

"Under the circumstances, I'll drive you over to his center myself, Rolf. You don't look too good, you know."

"I'll drive both of you there," Alvin volunteered. "I can't wait to hear what Lama Tsot says about this development, darling."

I called my secretary and let her know where we were going.

"Thanks, sweetie." I felt genuine gratitude towards Fila. Alvin guided us out to the car. All the way to the center, I felt like I was having a heart attack.

"What's wrong Rolf?" Fila was looking at the expression on my face.

"I can't breathe, my limbs don't seem to be working properly and my heart is racing," I complained.

"My God may be you're having a heart attack?" "Grab one of those paper bags, Rolf, and breath deeply into it," Alvin directed from the front seat.

"You're having a panic attack," he diagnosed. "I know. I have one myself everytime I meet someone new who I think might be my soulmate. And I always interpret the heart racing as love," he laughed. "Much to my misfortune, believe me."

I breathed in deeply, desperately trying to ground myself. Instantly, the heart palpitations stopped.

"Thanks, Alvin."

"If your parents do turn up, Rolf, just keep up the pretense for me, will you?" Fila asked as we drove into the center.

"Lie to my parents, Fila?" I couldn't believe her advice.

"It's the only thing to do. Otherwise the whole thing is too difficult to explain."

"You don't know my father. Because of our marriage and my agreement to become CEO of Enderby Developments, he'll think I've revoked my Buddhist status and am willing to come back into his business world, too."

"Let him think anything he wants. We don't want the Enderby Developments' succession problems to get out until you've got the board of trustees firmly in place."

"You don't have to wait, sweetie," I told Fila as she not only led me to Zot's center but sat down beside Alvin and I on the chairs outside his office. Zot's office door was closed and two young people were lined up on chairs ahead of me.

"I'll wait, Rolf," Fila insisted. "You don't realise how white your face is. I'm worried about you."

"What about you? That change in your father's will must have come as a complete shock."

"It did. Believe me, I'm still reeling. Imagine, father had more faith in our children than he had in either Drew or me. I can understand his doubts about Drew but I did nothing the past years but try and meet his perfectionistic business demands."

I patted her hand.

"I'll be fine, sweetie," I insisted. I tried to meditate. My first energy center, the fear chakra, kept trying to open right up and fire. The thought of a confrontation with my father over returning to his business was completely destroying the mindfullness I had taken 20 years to develop.

"This center is a hub of activity," Fila's voice brought me away from my dilemma.

I glanced around. The place was filled with people all right. Zot's fame as the Buddhist Lama who had won the Kentucky Derby was bringing in people from all over California. Chanting, drumming and cymbal clashing signalled the presence of a puja session in one of the rooms.

"That must be the visiting Lama from Tibet taking that group," I explained to Fila. Another group of Zot's students were working on sand sculptures in one corner of the large room. They looked bizarre with white, dust masks over their mouths to block out the dust from the sand.

"Whatever are those masked students doing Rolf?" Alvin asked.

"Making sand sculptures of the Buddhas and scenes of Buddhist history," I replied.

"That's a lot of work," Fila remarked. "Those sand sculptures are very detailed. What do the students do with them when they are finished?"

"Oh, they're destroyed and the materials recycled. The whole aim of the exercise is to get the detail of the sculptures into one's mind. In meditation, a student imagines a picture of the Buddha of choice. The more detail that goes into it's visualization the easier it is to merge with the energy. The exercise also teaches the students about the impermanence of life and anything in it."

"What a concept," Alvin commented. "The impermanence of life and everything in it. May be that's why my love affairs never result in anything permanent."

"What's that other group of students doing? They look completely bizarre." I followed Fila's stare.

"Oh, those students are making copies of Buddhist chants. See how they are using ink over wooden blocks to print out texts?"

"It's not just what the students are doing, Rolf, that's bizarre, it's what they look like. All of them have rings through some part of their anatomy."

"Oh, that's nothing to do with Tibetan Buddhism, darling," Alvin said. "That's just California. Haven't you noticed how young people are piercing their bodies these days? It's the latest trend. I was thinking of an eyebrow ring myself or perhaps a nose ring at the very least. And believe me, darling, you'd be surprised where some people have rings attached."

"My God."

"That your wife?" one of Zot's clients asked. "Why yes," I replied.

"She's not bad looking for someone over 30," he commented.

"Yes, she is holding up rather well," Alvin assured at the young college-type, fellow. He didn't resemble Zot's usual clients.

"Rolf, wat you do here," Zot was standing, looking surprised to see Fila and I.

"Another problem, Zot. But you take care of these clients first, will you. I don't want to cut in."

"You sure, Rolf?"

I nodded. He took the distraught looking woman at the front of the line into his office.

"So what brings you here?" I asked my new acquaintance.

"I need help, man," he replied. "My old man found out I've been taking some of the classes at this center. He's threatening to stop funding my university fees if I don't quit. I'm expected to become a rabbi not a Buddhist monk."

"Really," I sympathised.

"Who are those people, Rolf?" Alvin warned. They look like they don't belong in here at all?"

I glanced up at Alvin's words. He was pointing at a well-dressed, older couple asking one of the student groups for direction. I gasped as they headed over in our direction.

I stood up in disbelief as the older woman threw herself into my arms, hugged me close and broke into tears. I stared at her. Her back was hunched over. She had lost several inches in height. And her hands were gnarled with arthritis.

"Rolf, is that you?" I shuddered at the man's voice. He sounded just like he had 15 years before. I hugged the woman back, completely overcome by emotion.

"Your office said you would be here," the man said accusingly. "We went over there to see you and I managed to extract this address from your secretary. It wasn't easy, I can assure you."

"Hello, " I managed to extract myself from the clutch of the elderly woman. I put out my hand to the man. He ignored it.

"I see you haven't changed, Rolf," his voice dripped shame.

"Still frequenting with Lamas and Buddhist weirdos." he challenged, "and those people," he stared at Alvin.

"I was hoping that returning to the business world was a sign that you had finally regained your senses." He glanced around at Zot's center and the people in it with condemnation. I could tell he hadn't changed at all in 15 years.

"Johan," the woman challenged him. "Did you come all this way to alienate Rolf again? Isn't 15 years of silence enough for you?"

"Allow me to introduce my parents?" I managed to say to Fila. She was looking at them with a disbelieving stare.

"My wife, Fila," I gasped. "And her executive secretary, Alvin Carstairs."

"Are you one of these weirdo Buddhists, too, young lady?" demanded my father.

"You're pregnant, aren't you darling?" My mother was staring at Fila's expanding waistline. "Johan, we're going to be grandparents." She gave Fila a big hug.

"How long has she been suffering with arthritis?" I wondered.

"Is that why you married Geoffrey Enderby's daughter Rolf?" my father demanded. "Because you knocked her up?"

"And I thought my old man was out of sight," the young student next in line commisserated.

Zot's door opened and he came out with the young women he had been counselling. She was looking a lot better than when she entered his office.

"Rolf, who dese people?" he enquired.

"Allow me to introduce my parents," I stammered. "This is my father Johan Nordquist, and my mother Helen. This is Lama Tsot Rinpoche, a Buddhist Lama from Tibet."

Zot put out his hand. My father ignored him.

"How do you do, Lama Tsot?" My mother took Zot's outstretched hand. I realised with shock that my mother, at least, had changed in 15 years. The last time I had seen her she had firmly agreed with my father's decision to excommunicate me.

"I must have completely misjudged her," I thought, intense pain gathering around my heart center.

"Rolf has an appointment with Lama Tsot," Fila took command. "I'll drive you two over to our house. Rolf and I will be delighted to have you as our guests as long as you wish to stay, won't we, dear?"

"Go ahead of me, man," Zot's young client told me. "I can see why you need to see Lama Tsot."

"You'll promise you will come home immediately after your appointment?" Mother asked anxiously.

"Certainly, mother," I promised, giving her a hug. I had never felt so blown away by anything.

"The car is out this way," Fila led my parents towards the exit.

"Thank God Fila took them to the house," Alvin sighed. "What do you suppose he meant by 'those people,' Rolf.

"Oh, don't let that bother you, Alvin. My father is stuck back somewhere in the Nixon era."

"The Nixon era," Alvin commented. "I think it's more like the Tyronosaurus Rex era."

"How dey know where find you, Rolf?"

"It was Enderby, Zot," I stammered as Alvin and I went into his office. "He found out I was related to the Nordquists of Baltimore and he sent a letter to my father telling him of my marriage to Fila."

"Wat problem now Rolf?" he asked as Alvin and I came into the office.

"Fila expects me to go on with this lie, Zot. She wants me to pretend to my parents that our marriage is for real and that I'm going to run Enderby Developments forever. Shouldn't I tell my parents the truth, that this marriage is just a sham? A way for Fila to try and hold on to the management of her father's company."

"Your parents no understand, Rolf. You under no obligation tell dem anyting." I stared at Zot uncomprehendingly.

"Your mudder happy, Rolf. Find son she tink gone forever. And you be fadder soon. Your child need grandmudder. No need tell parents bout circumstances. Dey might tell baby someday. Baby not need know why dey brought into dis world. And watever going happen, happen soon wen baby born, anyway, you see."

"I thought I had everything under control Zot. I thought my parents were glad to get rid of me. I never even thought of my mother for 15 years. But now I just picked up her pain as she hugged me and how glad she was to find me. All that time she must have been missing me and suffering with arthritis."

"We do 'Phowa,' Rolf?" Zot directed.

I nodded. Alvin and I staggered over to the meditation pillows.

Zot contacted the Goddess Tara. I could feel her presence as I tried to reduce the energy in my fear chakra.

This is one hell of a 'Chod,' lesson, I complained mentally. I know a Buddhist is supposed to resist attraction and tolerate aversion, I bargained with Tara. But does everything one is trying to avoid have to happen at once. You know, I never expected to see my parents again. I never planned to be either a husband or a father. And you know the last thing I wanted to do in life was take part in business and commerce. That thought fired up my third energy center to do with self-worth. I doubled over in pain.

My fourth center, the heart center, fired up as I thought of my mother and father. I realised I had unresolved issues with both parents.

Damn, I cursed, I thought I left those issues behind years ago. My second center fired up. I realised it was firing because of relationship matters. All sorts of unresolved problems with relationships. A picture of Fila came into my mind. I acknowledged that despite her obsession with business, I was very attracted to Ms. Helmsley. Part of me couldn't wait until our baby was born and Ms. Helmsley might want to have sex again.

What a hope, I muttered. All she sees me as is a sperm deposit.

What a mess, I thought as my sixth center joined in on the fun. I realized I was reacting to the lack of control I was experiencing with my life. It was the first time in 20 years that I couldn't just abandon myself to Buddhist practices and my music.

"Rolf, you need stop fighting aversions," Zot had ended the 'Phowa.' "Dis situation bigger den you. Need accept challenges."

"Challenges, Zot?" I gasped. Every instinct I possessed made me want to run from Orange County, and never return.

"Maybe if I take the next plane to the Amazon?" I thought. "See how my trust is doing?"

"No leave California, Rolf," Zot had caught my thought. "Need do 'Chod' practice, instead. Need realise dat Buddhas have sent you challenge deliberately. Dere be opportunity fo you be force fo good here."

"How can I be a force for good here, Zot? The only force for good I'm connected with is my land trust in the Amazon. May be I need to go and find out how it's doing?"

"Rolf, you need tink bout wat you doing wit rest of dis life. Maybe you capable of mo dan being folk singer, helping Yanomami."

"But all I want is to go back to my music, Zot." I argued. "It's the one thing I've been successful at."

"Rolf, you need have mo self-wort. Why you successful now, at many tings. Green Tara like way you guiding Enderby Developments new direction. Mo socially responsible business practice. Green Tara say you help Fila, into be better sentient being. Say unborn child special baby. It Bodhicitta, come back dis world help sentient beings. Need fadder. Your mudder need son. Need resolve problem wit your own fadder. May be fadder's insurance business need help become mo socially responsible."

"Zot, I don't want to be around people that have no other interest but maximizing profits. I want to be with people who are more evolved."

"Green Tara say Buddhists not need gather all togedder and shine light to each udder. Say Buddhists need shine light where dere darkness. Be in place where can be most help. Tink dat in business fo you, Rolf."

"I'd say the most darkness is around your father, Rolf," Alvin intervened, "except for Drew Enderby, of course. He's like a one man force of darkness. But I don't suppose he's your problem. May be Baltimore is where you should be."

"Thanks, Alvin."

I staggered out of Zot's center. I realised it was going to take more than one "Phowa" session to settle the massive influx of emotions I was feeling.

I'm not used to all this emotion, I thought. For years, my emotions have been in nearly perfect balance.

I started as Fila was waiting for us on the sidewalk.

"How did it go, Rolf?" she inquired. "You still don't look too good."

"Lot's of unresolved stuff, sweetie," I explained. I tried to slow my whirling mind and my still fired up chakra centers. "Zot's got me working on it. Whatever did you do with my parents?"

"I put them in Father's bedroom, Rolf, with all the wedding pictures. They're freshening up for dinner. Michael is bringing their belongings from their hotel."

I braced myself for my father's inquistion.

More of Zot's words flowed into my mind.

"Green Tara want you help raise consciousness on dis planet. You need continue help Enderby Developments be mo socially responsible. You need continue help Fila become better sentient being. Tink of unborn child. Tink of mudder."

"This is one hell of a 'Chod' lesson," I stated to Fila and Alvin.

"How about we three go look at some baby things, darling?" Alvin asked Fila, staring at a baby store in front of us.

I thought of Zot's words.

"He was right before," I acknowledged. I forced myself to try a little 'Chod' practice.

"The baby is going to need a complete wardrobe, you know," Alvin suggested.

"He's right, sweetie."

"Sure Rolf," she gasped. "Dinner won't be for a couple of hours anyway."

"Zot's got me doing 'Chod' practice big time, sweetie," I explained.

"'Chod' practice?"

"Facing all the things you would rather avoid," I explained.

We went into the store. Alvin went on a shopping spree. I felt some amusement make it through the pain of all my energy chakras firing as Alvin took charge of the major purchases.

Fila left the baby purchases for delivery and we went back down to her car.

"Alvin and I will take your parents on a tour of Orange County tomorrow, Rolf," she volunteered. "It's the least we can do since it was my father that put your parents on to you again."

"You want my help, Fila?"

"No, the office is frantic for you to return, Rolf. Your secretary has been calling all afternoon."

"What about the Orange County projects?"

"They can wait until your parents go. I don't imagine your father will be here long. He seems just like my father, only interested in what's happening with his business. I've got the cable company installing an internet connection so your father's employees can be in constant contact with him through e-mail."

CHAPTER 21.

Hormones.

"No wonder Rolf took off to Nepal," Alvin sighed as I gave in to Rolf's father's command. We were in a long lineup for a phone at Disneyland.

"That man won't take 'no' for an answer," he commented. "Right in the middle of Disney's 'Tomorrowland,' he decides that you have to stop everything and contact Rolf, darling."

We finally reached the start of the line. I dialed father's old personal number.

"Rolf, thank God you're there," I sighed.

"What is it, sweetie?" he replied. "I can tell you're at your wit's end by the exasperation in your voice."

"It's your father. He's having a hissy fit. Suddenly after two weeks of Alvin and I driving him all over Orange County, he's not content to play tourist anymore. Your father demands that Alvin drive him to your office immediately so you can give him a personal tour of our Orange County projects."

"Exactly where are you, Fila?"

"In the middle of 'Tomorrowland,' Rolf. "Your mother is dying to see the rest of the theme park but your father has declared he's had enough. I can't seem to divert him to any of the other tourist attractions. He wants you. I've never seen anyone quite so obstinate. Your father is even more insistent on his own way than mine was."

"I know. Tell you what, Fila. Why don't you and Alvin drive them over to the new Elkhorn construction project. I'll meet you there rather than Alvin driving all the way over here."

"OK, Rolf. We'll meet you there, then."

It took Alvin over an hour to drive through congested traffic. Rolf was already waiting for us in front of the construction gate. He joined his parents in the back and we drove through the construction chaos to a parking space.

"There's a display suite down the way we can look at," Rolf pointed. Mr. Nordquist took off at a trot, his wife trying desperately to keep up with him. Rolf, Alvin and I followed behind.

"I must say that your father is more demanding than even Geoffrey at his worst," Alvin complained. "Why, when that man gets an idea in his head you simply have no choice."

"Believe me, I know, Alvin," Rolf commisserated. "He's always been like that."

"You're going to have to send me on another holiday after this, darling. Perhaps a Caribbean cruise. On one of those boats with a Norwegian crew. Have you ever seen how absolutely stunning those Norwegian ship's staff are. Like Norse Gods in white shorts and their little officer bars on their shoulders. May be that's where my soulmate has been hiding all these years."

"You've earned it, Alvin," Rolf agreed.

I watched Alvin glance around at the Elkhorn project in disbelief. A modern geriatric residence had arisen from the former parking lot of the Seniors' complex.

"Seventy percent of these suites have been sold already, Rolf?" Alvin commented. "What a blast! I want one of these myself, darling. As part of my retirement pension. After all I do for you, I'll deserve one of these for sure by the that time."

"Sure Alvin," I laughed.

How could Rolf have known that the luxury geriatric market was going to blossom? I thought. I felt myself looking at my handsome folk singer with awe. We had managed to find time to go over some of the Orange County projects I had once controlled. It was evident from the review that Rolf had drastically modified several of the large projects. I had managed to conceal my rage at his changing the projects without consulting me but when I calmed down and looked further my anger dissipated. It took me a while but I was forced to realise that the musician I had lured off of Laguna Beach was a financial genius. Projected financial statement after financial statement testified to enhanced profit and lessened environmental damage from his changes to my projects.

Rolf isn't the only one experiencing emotional turmoil, I acknowledged to myself as I noticed his father look startled as we viewed the impressive display suite in the new Elkhorn geriatric wing. My tour of the Elkhorn project woke up memories of how much I had counted on becoming chief executive officer of Enderby Developments. Flipping Elkhorn for a twenty-six million dollar profit was supposed to have been my piece de resistance, I recalled.

Rolf's right, Father was a fiend, I concluded.

"The majority of the units have already been sold, Mr. Nordquist," the young saleman informed Rolf's father. "Even though the new wing won't be complete for another five months. I think it's the ocean view that sells these places," he added. "And the number of medical services that will be available if needed."

I forced myself to acknowledge Rolf's better grasp than mine of new trends in the market.

May be it was just a fluke, I argued with myself.

Rolf's parents, Alvin and I stared at the expansive ocean view from the display suite. A flotilla of sail boats was in full view off Newport Beach. The sight of them bobbing up and down in the whitecaps of the blue ocean water gave me a funny feeling.

At least, those people have time for a little fun, I thought. Fear about the future struck me again. Why, with Oliver's birth, all the fun things I've denied myself for the last decade have been for nothing. I felt sick at the thought. Waves of nausea went through my system.

How could Rolf have better foresight than me? I wondered, gazing in admiration at the new Elkhorn wing. And to think that I wanted to turn this whole complex into a pharmaceutical company.

May be father was right about Rolf, I continued to acknowledge with shock. Father's words came back to me.

"Rolf is a natural, Fila. He seems to know in advance what potential or lack of it is present in every one of Enderby Developments' projects. And his way of handling staff is remarkable. Why, he has most of my executives and the board of directors eating out of his hand."

It's true, I acknowledged, sitting down on one of the luxurious overstuffed armchairs besides Rolf's mother.

How could I have been so lucky? I thought, remembering the day I had propositioned the man Alvin had recommended as a potential sperm donor off Laguna Beach.

"What did you say these units sell for?" Rolf's father was giving the young saleman an inquisition.

"Why $630,000.00," the young man replied. "And that includes an automatic upgrade to one of the specialized nursing care units if ever you require one. Five percent of the purchase price will get you into one of these units."

"This is a remarkable concept, Rolf," his father remarked. I could see Rolf nearly die in surprise at receiving praise from his father. "Why, I have lots of business associates who would be interested in this place. I'm going to keep it in mind, myself. Was this Enderby's idea to build this wing on to the original complex?"

"This complex is due to Rolf's foresight," I interrupted. "We were planning to bulldoze the other wing when Rolf found a way to save the original complex and maximize profits from the land."

"Really," Mr. Nordquist raised his eyebrows.

"I always knew you had real business talent, Rolf. That's why I could never understand your running off to join a foreign religious order. Thank God you've come back to your senses."

Rolf blushed a deep shade of red. I could tell he didn't want to debate the pros and cons of Tibetan Buddhism in the middle of the Elkhorn project display suite.

"What other projects have you got under construction, Rolf?" Enderby demanded.

"There's a shopping complex not far from here, if you would like to see it, father," Rolf stated. Mr. Nordquist nodded.

"Alvin, you drive Fila and my mother and I'll meet you there with my father."

That took another hour. I gasped as I drove into the almost completed shopping complex that Enderby Resources had been constructing for over a year. It didn't resemble it's original construction plans at all.

I reeled in shock. "Alvin, what's happened to this project?" I demanded as Rolf and his father drove up. "It's not at all like it's original design." I stared at the complex's bare, warehouse-like units with surprise.

"Rolf turned it into an 'anti-mall,' darling. Trendy, don't you think?"

"How clever of you, Rolf." I couldn't believe Mr. Nordquist's enthusiasm.

"That type of mall is the latest rage in Baltimore," he added.

"It is?" I gasped.

"The other 'anti-mall' in Orange County is solidly in the black, Fila," Rolf assured me. "And Enderby Developments already has a waiting list of retailers eager to set up shop in this one."

I noticed Rolf's father in furious conversation with Rolf's mother as we toured the rest of the construction site.

"That's enough touring for you, today, Mother," Rolf announced, as we caught up to them. He was looking at the gradually increasing swelling in her ankles. He walked us all back to my air-conditioned sedan.

"I'll show my Father Enderby Developments' new game-farm, Fila. The one that's going to grow it's own produce. You and Alvin drive mother home. We'll be there in time for dinner."

"The one that's going to grow it's own produce?" I said in amazement.

"Of course, darling," Alvin told me. "Just like Disney's Animal Kingdom in Florida. It's the latest trend in environmental consumerism."

"Oh, right, Alvin," Rolf's father agreed. "I've heard of the success of the new Disney complex. Growing some of the food helps considerably with the operating costs, I understand."

As Alvin drove towards the freeway I experienced some horrendous kind of growth period. I couldn't help thinking about the way Rolf seemed to be able to sense future trends that would be profitable.

He's more talented in a business sense than I am, I realised as I forced myself to admit the truth. Pain seemed to go through my entire bodily system, particularly around my heart.

If only Rolf wanted to stay on in my life, I caught myself daring to hope.

But that's impossible, I thought bitterly. He's only stayed on, as it is, because of the baby, I can tell. Just to establish joint custody like I agreed.

I'm so emotional, I acknowledged as Rolf's mother noticed me using a Kleenex to wipe my eyes.

It must be the pregnancy, I decided. I haven't felt right ever since the doctor confirmed the success of the fertility pills. Hormones are to blame, I decided, barely able to keep back tears at the thought of Rolf going off somewhere after the birth of our child.

"Johan just told me that he's tremendously impressed with both of you," Rolf's mother confided, considerable emotion evident in her voice.

"And so he should be," Alvin agreed from the front seat.

"I dragged Johan out here to California, you know. Johan had Rolf written off years ago but I never agreed completely with his assessment of our son. I always thought Rolf was just rebelling against his father's overbearing treatment. As soon as I saw your father's letter I knew there was hope. It was a good sign that Rolf had rejoined the business world. Johan only came with me because I threatened to divorce him if he didn't."

"What made him change his mind?" I reeled.

Johan's been using the last two weeks to evaluate you both, Dear. Even he can see what a wonderful pair you two make."

I stared at Rolf's mother in shock.

"You see, dear, Nordquist Insurance is diversifying. Johan told me that he wants to go into real estate as well as insurance. Johan just confided to me a few minutes ago that he was tremendously impressed with that Elkhorn complex's new wing. He wants both Rolf and you to go on our board of directors to help him decide which projects to invest in. What do you think, dear? Could you and Rolf commute back and forth to Balitimore?"

"Baltimore!" Alvin said in shock. "That's where that chap I had the fling with on the East Coast is moving. May be he's not as superficial as I thought. Maybe he has hidden depth. This must be synchronicity."

"Synchronicity?" I queried.

"It's the lastest buzz word of the New Age, darling. Things and people coming and going in your life that facilitate whatever you are trying to do to raise the consciousness, both personal and of the planet."

"Alvin," I protested. "Who did you pick that jargon up from?"

"From the chap I went to the East Coast with."

"Alvin," I advised. "That chap isn't superficial at all. Synchronicity sounds like a really deep concept."

"Really, I suppose it might be possible to give that relationship one more try," Alvin mused.

I thought of Rolf's mother's offer to put us on their board of directors.

That's all Rolf needs, I thought. An offer to go on his father's board of directors.

But you never know, an odd thought had suddenly occured to me. God knows I want to be involved in a business of some kind. And there's no way I'm going to be a lackey for Drew until his child is old enough to take command.

I suddenly found my vision blurring as tears ran down my face. I reached for the Kleenex box in embarrassment. I realised I was losing complete emotional control.

"I'm sorry, I don't know why I'm so emotional," I babbled to Rolf's mother. A strange mixture of despair, grief, longing and hope surged through me.

"Oh, don't worry, dear. I was like that during my pregnancy with Rolf. It's the hormone changes, that's all."

"I hope you're right," I told her. I tried to pull myself back together but sadness and anxiety kept permeating my mind.

Rolf's mother put her arms around me and hugged me closely.

"Please call me Mother," she encouraged warmly.

I grabbed a large clump of kleenex and allowed the tears to stream down my face.

"Don't worry, dear. It's just the pregnancy," Rolf's mother assured me as Alvin merged onto the freeway. "And of course the recent death of your father is undoubtedly still affecting you."

We reached the Newport Beach house and I went off to my bedroom. I threw myself onto the bed I was currently sharing with Rolf since his parents arrival and sobbed my heart out. When the sobbing finally subsided I picked up the white telephone on my end table. I couldn't believe what I was going to do.

"Lama Tsot," I recognized the voice that answered the phone.

"It's Fila Nordquist," I blurted. "I need to talk to you. Could I have an appointment first thing tomorrow?"

"Yes, of course," he answered. I noticed his attempt to pronounce the "r" in course correctly. "First ting. Is 7:00 ok?"

"I'll be there," I sighed.

I'm sure I've lost my mind, I told myself as I realized that my future depended on what a Buddhist Lama was going to advise me to do.

CHAPTER 22.

Buddhist Relationship Advice.

I left my early morning group of Tankha painting students as I spotted Rolf's wife waiting outside my office.

Dat good, I sighed as I glanced at my watch. Fila Nordquist early. I walked over and greeted her warmly. I glanced closely at her face as she rose to greet me. Her eye make up confirmed what I already thought—Dark circles, barely noticeable under the heavy cover.

She suffering, I confirmed mentally. Now may be be ready for growth.

"Wat problem, Fila," I asked.

"You promise you'll keep what I say absolutely confidential, Lama Tsot," she demanded. "Particularly from Rolf?"

"Of course," I assured her, working on my pronounciation of "r's." I was determined to become an influential speaker about Buddhist principles to Americans.

"I need develop perfect English," I sighed. "It very difficult," I acknowledged the struggle I was having.

I motioned Fila onto the meditation pillows by the altar in my office. She sat down on the low cushion with some discomfort.

"She getting close give birt," I acknowledged as Rolf's baby was making itself very known under the attractive maternity outfit the lady wore.

"Wat problem?" I asked her again. I noticed her complexion going beet red.

"I need help, Lama Tsot," Fila said. "I think I'm losing my rational mind."

"Normal during pregnancy," I tried to reassure her.

"It's more than that," she confessed. I could tell the lady was having great difficulty communicating her problem.

"You worried dat you have leave business, Fila." I tried to help her.

"Yes, of course," she answered. "It's not easy to lose multi-millions of dollars and the chief executive officership of a company that you've wanted for a decade. But it's something even more than that. This is very difficult for me and I need your advice." I nodded encouragingly.

"I don't want Rolf to leave me," Fila blurted. "After the baby is born. I just realised it."

"You want him stay on as boss, Enderby Developments?"

"No, it's even more than that. I don't want Rolf to go out of my life after the baby's birth."

"You fall in love wit Rolf?" I helped the lady put in words what was evident on her face.

"I can't believe it myself, but it's true, Lama Tsot. I suspect I fell in love with him early on in our relationship. I've been doing a good job of repressing my feelings until lately, I know, but something has happened. My feelings for Rolf have broken through with a vengeance, and they run very deep, I assure you."

I nodded.

"How Lama Tsot help?"

"You're one of Rolf's closest friends. Can't you tell me some way to get him to stay? There must be some way to get him to remain here, in California, at least. I can't bear to think of him running off to the Amazon."

"Why you love Rolf, Fila?"

"Why, because he's so wonderful, Lama Tsot." Fila told me that she had never know anyone that was so unselfish, caring, gentle, and unconditionally loving as Rolf. She said that he was even had a damn good business head, even if he did think that social responsibility should be more important than profit. Fila said that Rolf accepts her the way she is and that even she realizes that she is a pretty demanding person. Fila said that she appreciated that Rolf doesn't compete with her or try and tell her what to do like all the other men she had known in the past.

I nodded. "We do 'Phowa.' Ask Goddess Tara how possible fo you keep Rolf."

"I can't bear to think of him leaving, Lama Tsot," she added. "My life will be so empty without him. He's all I have now that father is gone."

"You try relax, close eyes, still mind, try ignore toughts of worry, grief, anxiety, fear, loss."

"I'll try, Lama Tsot."

I went into meditation and chanted the mantra that I knew would summon Green Tara.

Rolf's wife looked a little calmer as I felt the goddess's energy fill the room.

"What dis woman need do?" I asked the goddess. The answer came immediately. I ended the 'Phowa' session. Fila looked at me anxiously as I completed the ritual with a dedication to the benefit of all sentient beings.

"Buddhist dharma show way fo you," I advised her.

"You've thought of something?" she demanded.

"Buddhist dharma say if person want kind, caring, toughtful, unselfish, loving partner den dey must become like dat first. Den person be attracted to you."

Fila looked at me in amazement.

"You're saying that if I want Rolf to stay I have to become caring, unselfish, unconditional loving and thoughtful like him, Lama Tsot?"

"Exactly right. You good learner."

"That would require a complete makeover, as Alvin would say. I don't know if I am capable of such changes."

"You try. Trust Goddess Tara. We ask her help. Lama Tsot give you initiation, mantra, contact Green Tara. You change, you see."

"All right, Lama Tsot. I'm desperate enough to try anything."

I chuckled to myself. Rolf's proud lady was suffering. "Now she ready learn, grow," I said to myself.

I took Rolf's wife through the Green Tara initiation.

"What's the mantra to contact her?" Fila demanded as I ended the session.

I wrote out the mantra for her in phonetic English.

"OM TURE TUTARA TURA SO HA." I wrote.

You have initiation now. All need do, chant mantra, Green Tara come, anytime, anywhere. She promise.

"Thanks Lama Tsot." Rolf's wife sounded like she was reeling with heavy emotion.

"Mo bettah you set up altar in quiet place," I realised she might even accept further guidance. "Give small offerings, flowers, incense, rice, fruit. You ask Rolf. He be glad set up altar fo you," I assured her.

"Set up an altar?" she queried.

"Like dis one." I pointed to my small altar. "You find small table, Buddhist implements at New Age Centers, here, Orange County."

"That's a picture of my father on your altar, Lama Tsot."

"Dat right," I agreed. "Picture stay on altar 49 days from date of death. Lama Tsot, Rolf, do 'Phowa' ceremony fo your fadder, every Tuesday, 7:00 p.m."

"That's where Rolf goes. I was afraid he had some girlfriend somewhere. Thanks again, Lama Tsot." Fila placed some bills in my hands.

"You come wit Rolf, Wednesday night, 7:00," I advised. You join 'Phowa,' Tink you not release grief at fadder's death. Dat part of problem."

"I'll be here this week," she promised.

I gave gratitude in my heart to the Buddhas. I hadn't expected Rolf's wife to allow herself to feel her suffering enough to allow Buddhas to guide her.

"Wat next?" I wondered. "May be Mr. Enderby working from Buddha fields help his children. May be even Drew be asking Lama Tsot for advice next but not tink so?"

"Tink dat man need mo dan dis lifetime to start to grow."

CHAPTER 23.

Resolution.

"Phone Rolf," I frantically directed my housekeeper. "And get Gerald to drive me to the hospital right away. The baby's coming," I added.

Fear shot through me as I grabbed the bag Rolf had me make up for the hospital and walked out to my sedan. "The baby's early, just like Daphne's was," I thought. I was only officially seven months pregnant but Rolf was sure I was much further along than that.

"You probably didn't need fertility pills," he assured me as the baby got huge and dropped much before it was supposed to. "God, I hope he's right," I thought. The doctor was still holding on to his original birthdate forecast.

Gerald, our young driver, came flying out behind me and opened the door.

"Just be calm, Mrs. Nordquist," he advised. "We'll be at the maternity ward in no time at all."

"I hope so, Gerald," I replied. "These labor pains are getting awful close together."

I wonder if the baby will be a boy or a girl? I thought frantically. It doesn't really matter anymore, I knew. I recalled the changes to father's will.

Thank God, Oliver is doing so well, I thought. Daphne had phoned me that morning and said he had already gained three pounds and was sleeping through the night. Happiness gave way to fear as I thought about my present dilemma.

The question now was not what sex the baby going to be. It's what will Rolf do once our baby is in this world, I sighed. I hadn't dared to raise the question with him. He had said nothing about his plans once our child was born. I suspected he wasn't sure about what he was going to do himself.

"We're here, Mrs. Nordquist," I started as Gerald opened the car door. I came back to the present and moved myself into the wheelchair that Gerald was holding.

"Not a moment too soon," I gasped as my labor pains intensified fiercely.

"Take her right to the delivery room," the resident on duty ordered as he quickly examined me. "She's ready to give birth."

My worries about my husband gave way to excruciating pain as the baby decided it was time to enter this world.

"We're going to have to do a caesarian," one of the doctors advised in the delivery room. Then I felt myself losing consciousness as they injected something into my arm.

When I awoke my eyes were blurry as I tried to make out who was sitting next to my bed.

"The baby?" I questioned.

"It's a boy, Sweetie," Rolf quickly put my mind at ease. Seven pounds, six ounces. And healthy as a horse," he advised.

"Thank God," I sighed. "Whatever are we going to name him, Rolf?"

"Why, Zot, of course, after Lama Tsot." I was horrified. "Rolf, you can't name a baby Zot, even if this is California."

"OK, then we'll call him something starting with "Z", like Zachary, Zedekiah, or Zadok, and call him Zot for short."

"Let's give him the name Rolf for a first name? You can call him Junior if you want to use a nickname."

"Let's compromise, Miss Helmsley. "How about Rolf Geoffrey Johan Alvin Tsot Nordquist. I like that." The nurse brought in our baby. Rolf took it from her arms and gave him to me. She left and I put little Rolf to my breast. He immediately grasped onto the nipple and started to suck contentedly.

"Just like his father," Rolf laughed. Tears welled in my eyes.

"He looks just like you, Rolf. He's every bit as handsome."

We both stared at the baby in awe as he continued to suckle fiercely. After ten minutes, I switched him over to the other breast. He emptied that one and then went off into a well-deserved sleep.

"I'll put him in the crib, next to you, sweetie. Lucky boy. He gets to stay with you in this hospital." Rolf took him and gently transferred him to the crib.

"Here's Lama Tsot and Alvin," I smiled as our friends came bounding in to the room and stared at the baby.

"Wat you name him?" Lama Tsot demanded.

"Rolf Geoffrey Johan Alvin Tsot Nordquist," I stated, proudly. They both beamed.

"Congratulations, darling," Alvin gave me a big hug.

"He fine boy," Lama Tsot pronounced.

"You'll be the godfather, won't you, Alvin?" Rolf asked.

"Why, certainly," Alvin looked immensely pleased. "Who else is going to teach this little fellow the importance of style."

"We will need a blessing for the baby, Lama Tsot," Fila requested.

"Of course," Lama Tsot beamed. "In few days."

"I need to talk with you, Zot," Rolf requested.

"Here, now, wat problem Rolf?"

Rolf dragged the Lama out into the hallway. I sensed he wanted to ask him something about our marriage. Fear pulled at my heart.

"Alvin, go and see if you can hear what they are saying?" I ordered.

He winked and went out of sight behind the open door. I pulled myself into a sitting position. I knew I shouldn't but I was highly anxious. I ignored the pain.

"I can hear them fine, darling," Alvin reassured me. "They're in the waiting area directly across the hall."

"How do I ask Fila if I can remain in her life after the baby has been born," Alvin gave me a word for word repetition of what was being said?"

I gasped. My fear, pain and fatigue disappeared. My heart felt all warm and fuzzy.

"Wat you mean, Rolf?" I smiled at Alvin's imitation of Lama Tsot.

"You know she just contracted me for the birth of a baby, Zot. It's so embarrassing. I don't know what happened but I'm afraid I fell in love with her during the process. I think it even happened somewhere right near the beginning of our relationship. I tried to fight it but I know now in my heart that I don't want to be without her."

I crept back into the bed and motioned Alvin away from the door. My worst fears had been eliminated. I gave thanks to Lama Tsot and the Goddess Tara. I remembered Lama Tsot's advice.

"If you want attract kind, gentle, unconditionally loving husband den you need become kind, gentle, accepting, loving too," he had advised.

"It worked," I shouted joyously to Alvin. "It worked."

"Well, I'm glad it did, darling, whatever it was, even if I haven't the slightest idea what you're talking about."

"It be ok, I promise." I heard Lama Tsot advise Rolf loudly across the hallway. "I go now." His footsteps echoed down the hall.

Rolf came back into the room. He looked extremely nervous.

"How do you feel, sweetie? Can I get you anything?"

"Just kind of groggy, Rolf. I'll have a little water, please." He poured some for me and I gulped it down.

"I put my resignation in as chief executive officer," Rolf advised. "The Directors are going to set up a board of trustees to run Enderby Developments. They're going to use the names you suggested."

"Good, we don't need to be involved in it anymore, Rolf. I don't want you subjected to the whims of Drew and his latest love. Drew's become an absolute ego-maniac now that he knows his son is going to inherit Enderby Developments controlling stock."

Rolf nodded.

"How would you, Alvin and little Rolf like to go on a tour with me, sweetie?" I need to promote my Amazon Paradise CD immediately." He looked extremely anxious as he waited for an answer.

"Is that your way of asking me to remain in your life?"

"Yes, Miss Helmsley? What's the answer. Think you can get used to country music?" Tears filled my eyes. I reached out for him. He took me gently in his arms and kissed me tenderly.

"Now listen," he ordered. "I'm impressed with the way you took the birth of Oliver." Rolf told me that he was impressed that I gave up all my dreams of being CEO of Enderby Developments without a whimper, and that I had been nothing but unconditionally loving and supportive to Daphne. He told me that he knew that I didn't want to leave business all together, and that he had been in touch with his father and mother. He told me that he had agreed for both of us to go on the board of directors for Nordquist Diversified, as they were now calling their business. He said that we would have to attend board meetings twice a month and keep in touch constantly via phone, e-mail and fax, at least for starters.

"How about it?" he asked.

"You're going to schedule that in with your music tour?" I answered in disbelief.

"Why not. If Ted Turner and his wife can schedule both show business and business together why can't we? Particularly, if we've got Alvin along for the ride."

Rolf reached for me again.

"I take it, that's a yes, darling," Alvin said as we unwound ourselves several minutes later.

I nodded, tears streaming down my face.

"Alvin, you'll stay on as our Man Friday?" I asked.

"Well, I suppose I could consider it, darling. But I would like to draft my own job description, if you don't mind. I suppose part of my job is to help my godson?"

"If you're willing, Alvin," Fila replied.

"Well, I insist on the right to input on choosing his clothes. There's this new trendy baby clothes designer in Orange County. I just saw one of his designs. A space suit for kiddies. It would be perfect for little Rolf."

"We'll all have a veto on clothes, Alvin and yes, of course, you can write your own job description. You always have. And we'll double your salary?" I promised. After all, you are indispensible, you know."

Rolf broke into one of his songs from his Amazon CD album. His voice was full of joy.

"Well, I suppose I could try developing a taste for country music," Alvin agreed.

I glanced over at our baby. Little Rolf was cooing contentedly in his crib. Rolf handed him back to me again.

"This is what I'm meant to be doing with my life," I smiled, giving up all regrets about Enderby Developments chief executive officership as the baby looked at me with his big blue eyes. I knew he couldn't see yet but the little fellow was blinking at me intently with his eyes.

"He's doing the bonding thing we read about in Dr. Spock's book," I said to Rolf. All thoughts went out of my mind as I could feel a strong pull between my newborn baby's heart chakra, mine and Rolf's.

"Back and forth to Baltimore," Alvin commented. "Well, may be that's where my soulmate is."